# Now what?

"My Granny and I were doing just fine until I blabbed to you, Case. My *best friend*," Ned added.

Case tried to defend himself. "Hey listen, I didn't know my mom was going to—"

"Now what's going to happen?" Ned continued. "You don't know what you've started, Case." He was starting to sound more hopeless than angry.

Hopeless was worse, Case thought. "At least your Granny will get more help," he said, trying to point out the bright side. "That's what's important, isn't it? They won't mess with you, will they? As long as you keep on going to school?"

"That's what *you* think," Ned said gloomily "I've been through all this before—you don't know what you've started," he repeated. "Just wait."

# Some Friend

SALLY WARNER

SCHOLASTIC INC.

New York   Toronto   London   Auckland   Sydney
Mexico City   New Delhi   Hong Kong

★

*I thank Valerie Mack of Philadelphia's Department of*
*Human Services. Any inaccuracies are, of course, my own.*

For
Todd Jackson, my sister,
and
Todd Warner, my brother.
Some friends!

ISBN 0-439-07846-6

Text copyright © 1996 by Sally Warner.
Cover art copyright © 1996 by Mark Elliot.
All rights reserved.
Published by Scholastic Inc., 555 Broadway, New York, NY 10012,
by arrangement with Alfred A. Knopf, Inc.
SCHOLASTIC and associated logos are trademarks and/or registered
trademarks of Scholastic Inc.

12 11 10 9 8 7 6 5 4 3 2 1                    9/9 0 1 2 3 4/0

Printed in the U.S.A.                    40

First Scholastic printing, April 1999

# ★ CONTENTS ★

# 1

# THE HILLS OF
# PHILADELPHIA

Case cleared his throat and tried again: *"At the sound of the beep..."*

"Moo like a sheep!" Lily interrupted, breaking into giggles. She hugged herself and rolled on the floor.

"Cut it out," Case said, frowning. He rewound the tape and got ready to begin again. "Anyway, sheep don't moo, they baa. Don't they teach you anything in first grade? Now I've got to start all over. I want it to be done when Mom gets back, to surprise her."

"She'll be surprised enough we have an answering machine. Who's going to leave us messages?" Lily asked.

"Lots of people. You never know. And anyway, it was free—Buddy got that new one. I'm going to try again, so keep quiet." Buddy was their friend, neighbor, and landlord. The old house they all lived in had been divided into two apartments, and Buddy's was the one downstairs.

"I'll be quiet as a sheep," Lily promised.

"That's what I'm afraid of," her brother said gloomily. "Okay, here goes: *Hi! This is the Hills. I mean, these are the Hills. Please leave a message at the sound of the beep.*"

"BEEP!" Lily squawked, grabbing the telephone. Case held it away from her with one hand and rewound the tape.

"We might leave that in, just so people know you live here too. Now let's listen. Pretend you're some guy who just called, but we aren't in."

"Okay," Lily said. She lifted an imaginary phone and said, "Ring, ring!"

Case pressed the message button, and they listened to his recorded voice in silence. "You sound like a girl," Lily said, when the message was finished. "Your voice is all high and squeaky when you say, *These are the Hills.*"

"I think I sound like a bird," Case said, disgusted.

Lily thought a moment. "A *girl* bird," she agreed.

4

"But I don't really sound like that, do I?"

"Not usually. Sometimes you sound almost like a grownup. Like Daddy, when he calls."

"Let me try again," Case said. "Lower, this time. You say 'beep' when I point to you, Lily. Got it?" She nodded, solemn. The tape started. *"Hi,"* Case said in his lowest voice. *"You have reached the Hills of Philadelphia."* Lily started to giggle again but clamped her hands across her mouth when Case glared at her. *"Please leave a message at the beep,"* he continued, then pointed at Lily. "Now," he whispered.

"What?" she whispered back.

"Say 'beep'!" he hissed at her.

"I can't say it," Lily hissed back. "Not now. I'm not in the *mood.*"

*"BEEP,"* Case finished. He turned to his sister. "That's going to sound really stupid on the tape."

"Who cares?" Lily cried. "No one's going to call us up anyway! They never did before, did they?"

"Well, that's the whole *point.* We never had an answering machine before, so how would we know if anyone called or not?"

"You're going to be sorry you ever let Buddy give us that thing," Lily said, scowling. "And anyway," she added with a sniff, "it sounds dumb to say we're the Hills of Philadelphia. Philadelphia doesn't even *have* any hills, not around here. So you're the stupid one, Case, not me."

"I never said *you* were stupid," Case began, but he was talking to an empty room. Lily had stormed off, slamming the bathroom door behind her—as usual.

It was eight-thirty at night, and Case and his mom had just finished washing the dishes. Lily was fast asleep, and the apartment was finally quiet.

Mrs. Hill was often tired after working all day at the old bookstore. Tonight, though, she and Case shared a sense of excitement over their new answering machine. After wiping her hands with a blue plaid dish towel, she leaned forward to listen to the recorded message one last time. Case pressed the button. His voice sounded, low and clear. *"Hello. You have reached the Hills. Please leave a message when you hear the beep."*

"Casey, it's perfect." Mrs. Hill said, beaming. "You sound so natural! And how did you ever figure this machine out? It would have taken me days."

"Buddy taught me. It wasn't so hard," Case said, giving the machine a little pat.

"Did Lily help too?"

"Yeah," Case said, grinning. "She shut herself in the bathroom."

"Well," Case's mother sighed. "So now we have an answering machine. I can't believe it. We really should pay Buddy something for it, Case..."

"He said no, but I'll do some extra chores or something. Don't worry."

"I guess this means we'll have to return all phone calls now. No excuses," Mrs. Hill said with a grin and a shrug.

"Yeah, but Mom, think of all the great messages we're going to get. It'll be worth it. I can hardly wait!"

"Anyway, I'm glad you didn't make one of those silly tapes, Case. I hate calling someone up and getting one of those. I never know what to say. Your message is nice and dignified, honey."

Case nodded, pleased. "Dignified. That's us."

His mother laughed and ruffled his hair. "Well, some of the time at least."

"Like when we're asleep," Case added.

"Excellent example. Now, into bed, Mr. Hill. At the sound of the beep!"

# 2

## ONE LITTLE NUT

"Hi, Mrs. Hill? This is Bess Greenough. I'm the first-grade room mother this year—Lily's class. Lucky me, ha ha! We should get your Lily and my Daisy together to play. The little flowers, ha ha! Anyway, I'm calling about the cupcakes. Lily told us about her birthday tomorrow, and we're all thrilled about the special treat, but I wanted to warn you about our healthy-snacks policy. You can't start good habits too early, can you? And Stevie Braddock can't have nuts. Thanks again, and happy birthday to sweet little Lily. Bye-bye!"

"Oh, sweet little Lily," Case called out, poking his head into the bedroom she shared with her mother, "Mom wants to talk to you. Now! She's in the kitchen." Lily bounced up from her bed, scattering tiny glittering doll clothes everywhere, and pushed past her brother.

Case headed toward his own bed, which was basically his whole room. It wasn't anything like the big bedroom he'd had all to himself in Cherry Hill. In Philadelphia, the Hills' apartment was small, but there was an alcove at one side of the living area that was Case's private space.

Right after they'd moved in the previous summer, Mrs. Hill had sewn a red-and-white-striped curtain that Case could pull shut. When he did this, he felt as though he were living inside a little circus tent. His bed filled most of the alcove. A little painted table crammed in at the head of the bed held his favorite books and his clock radio. Case's drawings covered the walls. But even with the striped curtain pulled shut and the radio playing, he could hear the conversation in the kitchen.

"Lily, what on earth is going on?" his mother was saying. "There's a message on the answering machine saying it's your birthday!"

"I'm seven?"

"No, Miss Hill, it's *not* your birthday and you

9

know it. Your birthday is in July, and this is only March."

"But that's no fair! I never get a school birthday. Other kids get one, and their parents bring in treats for the whole class, and everyone sings to them."

"So you told the teacher it's your birthday tomorrow?"

There was a pause; then Lily said, "Maybe I did. I can't remember, actually."

"And you told them I'd bring in cupcakes?"

"But don't forget Stevie Braddock can't eat nuts. He'll swell up like a balloon and maybe pop!"

"Lily, it's eight o'clock at night. When were you going to tell me about this?"

"I don't know." Lily thought a moment. "Before bed?"

There was a longer pause; then her mother said, "Lily, I'm going to do it. Why, I don't know, and what healthy cupcakes are I don't know, but this year you can have a school birthday. My birthday's in the summer too, and I remember what that was like. But from now on no fibbing, and no signing me up to do things without checking first. Promise?"

"I promise, I promise! But don't make them *too*

healthy, okay? Mrs. Greenough makes these crumbly ones that taste like you're eating dirt. Even Daisy won't eat them."

"These will only be medium healthy," her mother promised.

"And Mommy? Maybe we could put in one little nut—so Stevie Braddock could swell up just a little? I never saw that."

"Lily, no nuts! That could be very dangerous for him, *very*. For goodness sake."

"I only meant a *little* nut," Lily said, pouting, "just for fun. But I guess singing's enough."

"Lily..." Her mother's voice held a warning note.

"I mean singing and cupcakes are fine," Lily said hastily. She thought for a moment, then added, "I wonder what Case is going to get me."

"Go ahead and ask him, Lily. I'd be interested to hear what he says."

"So are you actually buying her a present, when it's not even her birthday?" Ned asked the next morning during the city bus ride to Ben Franklin Middle School. Cold air seeped into the bus every time the long doors wheezed open. Case and Ned gripped sticky poles to keep their balance as the crowded bus lurched forward. Case stared at Ned's bony wrist, then averted his eyes. Ned's clothes were always a little too short—or a little too big. They never seemed to fit him right.

"Nah. That's carrying things too far," Case said. "I told her not to push her luck. Anyway, she'd just expect more loot next July when her *real* birthday comes. But I did help Mom make the cupcakes. The helper gets to lick the bowl," he pointed out. Ned shook his head in wonder. His glasses slid down his nose, and he pushed them back up almost automatically.

Ned lived alone with his grandmother. He had moved to Philadelphia years ago, when his mother couldn't take care of him anymore. Ned had never known his father. Since he had never lived with any brothers or sisters, he was always amazed at the confusion one little girl could cause. "Well, my Granny would never do that," he said. "Stay up late making cupcakes for my class, I mean. Especially if I told a lie to get them."

"Knowing Lily, she believed it was going to be her birthday, once she said it," Case tried to explain.

Ned shifted his backpack, trying to get more comfortable. He lowered his voice and continued, "I'm just saying Granny never would have, that's all. Not that she even could, now."

"What do you mean?" Case asked.

"Well, she's kind of—kind of tired a lot. It's like she's worn out. It's hard for her to go upstairs, even. So she got me to move her bed down to the living room," he added in a rush. He looked sideways at Case, as if checking his reaction.

"She sleeps in the living room now?" Case asked, shocked. Ned's Granny was famous for never letting anyone even *sit* in her living room. Every room in her house was tidy, but her living room—with lace on every satin armrest and cellophane still wrapped around each teetery lamp—was spotless. The Ryans' living room always looked as if it was waiting for something to happen, or waiting for someone important to visit, Case had always thought.

"She's only sleeping downstairs for now," Ned said, "just until she feels better. That's how come I haven't asked you over for a while," he added, looking embarrassed.

"Oh," Case said. *I didn't even notice,* he thought,

feeling a little guilty. Well, he figured he had a lot more going on in his life than Ned did.

"Granny doesn't want people seeing everything all raggedy."

"Who cooks?"

"Me," Ned said, as though it was nothing. "I do okay for us both. I even make Granny's lunch before I leave for school."

"But who washes the clothes? Who cleans the house?"

"It's not that hard, Case," Ned said, blushing a little. "It's not like you have to feel all sorry for me or anything. I was only trying to say there's no way my Granny would ever have made twenty cupcakes in the middle of the night, even if she wasn't worn out."

"Thirty-four cupcakes," Case corrected him.

"Whatever."

The doors eased open in front of Ben Franklin, and Case and Ned stepped off the bus and into the icy air. Although it was still morning, some of the kids around them had already started eating their lunches; potato chip bags and sandwich wrappers scudded up against the grimy steps leading to the battered front door. Case and Ned trudged up

14

the stairs and—without another word—went their separate ways. The warning buzzer sounded. Another school day was about to begin.

"Mom," Case said later that night, after his mother had quizzed him on his spelling list, "what happens to kids when there's nobody to take care of them?" He settled back cross-legged into the apartment's one big comfortable chair. His mother was seated at the kitchen table, feet up on another chair, her mug of tea nearby. She gazed at him, concerned.

"You mean like when somebody dies? A parent? Oh Case, you don't have to worry about that. If I died, your Aunt Nina and Uncle Charles would take care of you and Lily both. Until your father gets out of prison anyway, and probably even after that," Mrs. Hill said, her mouth pulled up tight. She ran her hand back through her short curly hair.

Case hated it when his mother tried to read his mind—and he especially hated it when she brought up the subject of his father. *"Mom,"* he said, "I'm not even talking about that. Other people have problems too, you know. Everything's not us all the time. It's *Ned* who's the one!" he blurted out. Right away he was sorry.

"Ned? Why, what's wrong with Ned?"

"Nothing's wrong with him. It's his Granny, I think."

"Mrs. Ryan? Case, what are you talking about?" His mother's tired face creased with this new worry.

"I probably shouldn't say anything. He said everything's fine." Case picked at the frayed cuff of his jeans.

"But?"

"But, well, when Ned was talking this morning, it kind of sounded like he was taking care of his Granny, not the other way around. He's cooking and everything. So I was just wondering what would happen..."

"If she were to die?"

"Well, yeah. Would they let him stay in that house? I know he can take care of himself. He's a pretty good cook, Mom," Case added, as if trying to convince her.

"There's more to it than that, Case," his mother said gently. "Ned's only what—twelve?"

"Same as me. He'll be thirteen in November."

"I know you can't live alone when you're twelve. Just how sick is Mrs. Ryan, anyway?"

The concern in her voice scared Case. "How should I know?" he said, jumping to his feet. "Maybe she's not sick at all. Ned said she was just kind of worn out. *You* get worn out. So do I. In fact, I'm worn out from this whole conversation right now."

"Case, calm down. I only—"

"I'm sorry I even asked about it! It's none of our business, Mom. So don't..." His voice trailed off.

"Don't what, Casey?"

"Just don't *do* anything. Okay?"

# 3

## WHAT ABOUT NED?

"Thanks a lot, Case. Some friend you turned out to be."

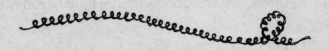

Lily was tired and had to be coaxed up the steep flight of stairs, but Case was eager to find out if there were any messages waiting on their new machine. He ran ahead of the others and let himself into the dark apartment. The red light glowed—someone had called! Case pressed the button on the answering machine and listened.

"Mom!" He threw his backpack across the room. The bag landed with a heavy thud. Ned's bitter recorded voice echoed in the dark apartment as Mrs. Hill and Lily struggled through the front door.

"Hush, Lily. What's the matter, Case?" his mother asked him, turning on the overhead light.

"Listen to this," he said, furious. He rewound the tape and played back Ned's angry message. When the message was finished, he turned to face his mother. "You promised you *wouldn't,* Mom. What did you do, exactly?"

"Casey, I didn't promise a thing," his mother began, her voice patient.

"But I told you not to go messing everything up."

"It's not the same thing at all, Casey. And you watch how you talk to your mother, young man. This is serious. Mrs. Ryan needs help." Mrs. Hill shrugged off her coat, draping it over a shiny chrome kitchen chair, then went over to the sink to wash her hands.

"How do you know? You're not the mom of the world!"

"I know she needs help because I went over there at lunch, Case. No one came to the door, so I let myself in with the spare key." The Hills sometimes fed and walked Lacy, the Ryans' little dog, when Ned and his Granny took the train to visit her sister in New York—so they knew where the Ryans' key was hidden.

"Yeah?" Case said, not wanting her to go on.

"You sneaked in?" Lily asked, eyes wide, fatigue forgotten. She curled up in the chair next to the phone as if ready for a story. "Weren't you scared?"

"No, baby. Mrs. Ryan was very glad to see me. She needed help getting to the bathroom." Mrs. Hill rummaged in a cupboard and emerged with a big can of tomato sauce.

"Mom!" Case didn't want to hear this.

Lily frowned, confused. "You helped her go potty? But Mommy, she's an old lady."

"Sometimes people get sick, and they get weak. They can have trouble walking, so they need someone to help them."

"Ned helps her," Case pointed out stubbornly.

"Casey, Ned leaves for school at seven-thirty and doesn't get home until almost four. That's more than eight hours."

"She has to wait all day to go potty?" Lily asked, horrified. She expected bathrooms to be available to her on a moment's notice, no matter where she was. "What about eating? Wouldn't she starve?"

Mrs. Hill laughed, came over to the chair, and hugged her. "Ned wouldn't ever let his Granny starve," she said, dropping to her knees. "He'd left her a peanut butter sandwich and a can of root beer."

"Peanut butter is very good for you," Case said. "It's got a lot of nutrition in it."

"That's not the point, Case. The point is, they need some help."

"Like what kind?"

"I told Mrs. Ryan I'd call around to see about home care for seniors. Some sort of government service, maybe."

"You mean she'd go into an old ladies' home? But what about Ned?"

"Not go into a home, Case. Someone comes into the person's home and helps out. With laundry, baths, meals, and so on."

Case looked as though he didn't believe it, but before he could argue anymore, Lily said, "So everything will be fine. What's for dinner, anyways?"

Mrs. Hill laughed and got to her feet. "Spaghetti, baby. It'll be ready in twenty minutes— and don't you *dare* fall asleep before then. You watch her, Case, and make sure."

Case called Ned's house that night while his mother was keeping Lily company at bath time.

Ned's phone rang eight times before anyone answered it.

"Yeah, hello?" Ned's voice sounded hurried.

"Hi, Ned? It's Case."

"Oh." There was a long pause.

Case took a deep breath. "Hey, my mom went over to your house today, at lunch. I didn't know it."

"But you told her about Granny."

"Yeah, yeah. I told her. It was kind of an accident, Ned."

"Well, it *kind of* goofed everything up, Case," Ned said, sarcastic. His tone of voice startled Case; Ned almost never got mad at him. Ned admired him. Case was practically Ned's only friend at Ben Franklin, so Ned needed him, even, and Case liked it that way. "Now Granny's all talking about the city sending someone over to help her," Ned was saying. "But *I'm* helping her. I'm doing just fine, or I was until you butted in."

"But if the city has people who'll come over and cook for her, and help her go to the bathroom, and stuff..."

"Wake up, Case! It's not that simple," Ned said, still sounding angry. "They'll be poking around, changing everything."

"But Ned, maybe if you got some help, you could do more stuff at school. Stay late for clubs and sports and everything."

"I don't want to do any of that stuff. I just want to take care of my family!"

"But your Granny—"

"You don't even think I *have* a family, do you Case?" Ned said. His words seemed to tumble over each other in their rush to get out—as if he had been waiting a long time to say them. "Just because my family's not all perfect like yours, with a mom and sister and everything, doesn't mean it doesn't count."

Case listened to a howl from the bathroom. His mother was drying Lily's hair. *Ned knows my dad is in jail,* he thought, twisting the cord angrily. *We don't even have our own house anymore—we had to sell it! Our car, too. Not to mention Lily being all goofed up. So how can he say we're perfect?* Case finally spoke: "Yeah, well."

"My Granny and I were doing just fine until I blabbed to you, Case. My *best friend*," he added.

Case tried to defend himself. "Hey listen, I didn't know my mom was going to—"

"Or maybe we aren't such good friends after all," Ned interrupted.

"What's that supposed to mean?" Case asked. Ned hesitated. Case could almost see him chewing his lower lip, the way he did whenever he got nervous. "Come on," Case insisted. "What do you mean?"

"Like at school!" Ned blurted out. "Does that ring any bells?"

"Yeah, well," Case said reluctantly, but he winced. He liked Ned and everything, but Ned really had a problem at school. Ned was the kind of kid other kids either ignored or laughed at. They didn't laugh at him in front of Case anymore. But maybe Ned didn't know Case had done at least that much for him, anyway.

"Now what's going to happen?" Ned was saying. "You don't know what you've started, Case." He was starting to sound more hopeless than angry.

Hopeless was worse, Case thought. "At least your Granny will get more help," he said, trying to point out the bright side. "That's what's important, isn't it?"

"Yeah, that's what's important," Ned said, but his voice sounded hollow. "We can just forget about me, I guess. Might as well."

"But *you're* okay," Case said, starting to get

24

scared. "They won't mess with you, will they? As long as you keep on going to school?"

"That's what *you* think," Ned said gloomily. "I've been through all this before—you don't know what you've started," he repeated. "Just wait."

# 4

# NORMAL

"Mrs. Hill? My Granny says it's okay to come over tomorrow morning. She says she likes chicken fine, and also chocolate chip cookies. Oh, this is Ned."

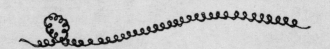

The Hills spent Sunday at the Ryans' house on Front Street. They walked over early, jackets pulled tight against the wet wind that blew across the Delaware River. The blue Ben Franklin Bridge looked dull against a cloudy sky. Mrs. Hill swung a plastic bucket full of cleaning supplies, and Case and Lily struggled to carry a Styrofoam cooler between them.

"Just give it to me," Case said. "You're too short to help carry this."

"I am not. Maybe you're too tall! Anyway, I've got just as many arms as you."

"Yeah, but they're too far down. All the food is sliding around, getting squashed."

"You can't squash chicken. Duh!"

Case gave up arguing with his sister. He tried not to imagine how foolish they looked, lurching down the sidewalk. *Lucky no one else is dumb enough to be out,* he thought, peering around. *They're all inside, doing normal things.* It started to rain.

"Almost there!" Mrs. Hill sang out.

Ned opened the door, holding back Lacy—a small, black, yapping pile of tangled fur—with one skinny sneakered foot. Case avoided Ned's eyes.

"Hello, Ned," Case's mother said, giving him a little hug. "Thanks for having us."

"Hi," Ned mumbled. "Lacy, shut up! Sorry," he said to the Hills as he closed the door. The little hall smelled funny, Case thought, like a mixture of old food and medicine. Vitamin pills, maybe.

"I brought a hairbrush for Lacy," Lily announced, pulling one out of her pocket. "I'll make her beautiful again."

"Lily!" her mother said. "That's *yours.* I'm sure Lacy has her own brush."

"Somewhere," Ned said, looking around the hall as if it might be there.

Case looked around too. Jackets were piled on top of muddy boots, and stacks of mail leaned against the wall. Ned was watching him, and Case suddenly had the feeling he was snooping, somehow.

"Neddy?" a cracked voice called from behind the folding screen that hid the living room from the hallway. "Are they here yet?"

"We're here, Mrs. Ryan, all ready for you to put us to work," Mrs. Hill said.

"Oh," Ned's grandmother said, suddenly confused. She was sitting stretched out on the sofa, surrounded by pillows. She twisted her hands in the blanket that covered her legs. "I don't know what—"

"Now, don't you worry about a thing," Mrs. Hill said softly, sitting down next to her. "I'll figure it all out. Then after today it'll be easier, I promise." She installed Lily next to Mrs. Ryan and gave them a box of graham crackers and the television remote control. Lacy immediately started drooling and stared fixedly at Lily.

"Lacy likes me," Lily said happily. "Hey, Case, she likes me!"

But Case and Ned were already busy on the tiny top floor of the house, Ned's room, with a big plastic garbage bag. They emptied wastebaskets and tossed all the dirty laundry down the narrow stairs. The washer and dryer were in the basement.

"If you even *think* it could be dirty, toss it," Case's mother called up to them. "And strip the beds."

"I can tell if my clothes are dirty or not, don't worry," Ned muttered, loud enough for Case to hear. "I've been doing this all my life, practically."

"She didn't mean—"

"Hey, look," Ned said, sounding embarrassed. "I was going to clean this up today even if you guys didn't come. But the important thing is how well I take care of Granny, right? Not how clean my room is."

"Yeah," Case said, trying to reassure him. "I mean, you should see what my bedroom used to look like." *When I had a bedroom,* he thought.

By lunchtime, things were a little easier between Case and Ned. The morning had passed quickly and noisily: Lacy's excited barks mixed with the equally excited voice of a Sunday morning television preacher. Lily and Mrs. Ryan watched, wide-eyed. "How come he's yelling?" Lily asked. She had never seen such a thing before.

The washing machine thudded, and the dryer squeaked. Ned's radio played in his room as he and Case washed windows and wiped shelves clean. Mrs. Hill's portable radio crackled in the kitchen as she sorted shelves and cleaned out the refrigerator.

Lunch was a picnic on the living room floor. Mrs. Hill spread out a tablecloth and opened plastic containers full of things she'd prepared the night before.

By midafternoon, the Ryans' house was peaceful, clean, and quiet. "Bye now," Mrs. Hill said, giving Mrs. Ryan a hug. The last graham cracker crumb had been vacuumed from the rug, and Lacy lay panting, silky and round, in front of the now dark television set.

"Oh, darlin', I'll never be able to thank you enough," Mrs. Ryan said.

"You don't need to thank me one little bit, Hazel. We were happy to help. That's what friends do! Now, let's give you some rest."

The Hills waved goodbye to Ned from the sidewalk. The sun had come out, and so had lots of people; Case held the cooler high in front of him so it wouldn't jostle anyone on the walk home. Lily had lost all interest in helping to carry it. Case watched her skip along ahead of him while holding her mother's hand. He just hoped no one he knew would see him. He must look ridiculous!

Ned called Case that night. "Hey, thanks," he said, gruff. "That wasn't so bad after all, you guys coming over. Granny's asleep already. We ate some of that food your mom left for supper."

"That's good," Case said.

"Granny said this lady is coming over tomorrow, when I'm at school. From the city—to see if everything's all right."

"Yeah?"

"Maybe it'll go okay, now that everything looks all normal and everything. They like stuff to look clean, I remember that much. I mean, *I* was keeping things clean, I just got a little behind. But maybe they'll leave us alone after tomorrow."

"You had a lady from the city come by before?" Case asked.

"Not this city," Ned said. "In Texas. When I was a kid. You know, living with my mom?"

"Oh, yeah," Case said.

"That's when I was six. But then they decided I should come live with my Granny," Ned said, leaving out the details. "They like to move kids around, I guess. You know, like chess." Ned was a chess player and was always trying to teach the game to Case, who had tried and tried to learn.

"Yeah," Case said. "But you're glad, aren't you? You like it here?"

"It's okay," Ned said. "My Granny took care of me, and now I'm taking care of her. If they'll *let* me."

"You're doing great," Case told him. "She looked very—sturdy."

"She's pretty tough," Ned agreed, happier. "Anyway, thanks. It wasn't so bad today. I guess I'm sorry I got all mad."

"That's okay. I shouldn't have gone telling everyone your business."

"It was just your mom," Ned said, forgiving.

"Maybe you'll have more time now, for fun," Case said, thinking of all the work they'd done that day. No wonder Ned hadn't been able to do anything lately!

"Well, maybe," Ned said, cautious again. "I sure wish I could be here when that city lady comes tomorrow, though, to explain stuff to her. Let's just keep our fingers crossed about all this."

"Okay," Case said. "But I'm sure everything will go great."

# 5

## IN SPITE OF EVERYTHING

"Mrs. Hill? This is Ellen Rosen, from the Philadelphia Corporation for Seniors. I just wanted to follow up with you and tell you we've made our preliminary visit to the Ryans. So we're evaluating the situation. Thanks for alerting us."

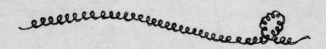

"Alert! Alert!" Lily called out as she chased baked beans around her dinner plate with a fork. She stabbed one.

"Lily, baby, you can use a spoon with those beans," Mrs. Hill said. Lily ignored her.

"Well," Case said, "I think it sounds dumb, having a corporation for old ladies."

"Senior citizens," his mother corrected him. "And it's for men, too."

"Whatever. It sounds like a factory or something. And what is that visiting lady going to do, anyway? What does she mean, 'evaluating the situation'? What situation?"

"I think she means she'll see how much help Mrs. Ryan needs. For instance, I think she could probably get around a lot better if she had one of those metal walkers in the house. She could get to the kitchen, the bathroom."

Lily looked up from her plate. "Ned's glasses are broken. He's got silver tape holding them together, did you see?"

"So what?" Case asked.

"So maybe that lady will buy Ned some new glasses," Lily said. "And a leash for Lacy!"

"The Official Corporation for Philadelphia Dogs does that," Case said, sarcastic.

"Oh," Lily said. She turned back to her baked beans.

"Maybe someone *will* help Ned buy new glasses," Mrs. Hill said, tossing the salad.

"Mom," Case said wearily, feeling like an old expert, "Ned's been through all this before. No one's going to help him. Ned says kids just get moved around like chess pieces. I guess that makes grownups feel like they're doing their jobs or something."

35

"There's a little more to it than that, Casey. I know Ned hasn't had an easy time of it, but things have worked out pretty well for him so far, in spite of everything, wouldn't you say?"

"I guess," he said, reluctant to admit that maybe his mom had been right after all about helping.

Case and Ned sat in the noisy cafeteria at Ben Franklin Middle School. A big eighth-grade girl screamed at her boyfriend, who pretended not to hear; speckled green plastic trays clattered onto sticky tabletops.

The two boys brought their lunches from home, but they bought drinks at school and ate in the cafeteria when it was cold outside. Case's straw slurped air from the bottom of his waxy milk carton. Ignoring the sloppy joe that had skidded to a stop—sloppy side down—in the middle of their table, he unwrapped a second sandwich.

"So I told Mr. Branowski I might be able to join the chess club after all," Ned was saying. Mr. Branowski was Ned's math teacher, and the chess club coach, too.

"When's it meet?"

"Thursdays, after school. Kids play the rest of the week, but that's on their own."

"Sounds like fun," Case said, trying to imagine it. "That could be like a whole different life for you." All winter, Ned had rushed home right after school to take care of his Granny. Case pulled his folding chair in as close as he could to the table. Behind him, two boys had started shoving each other, pretending to fight. They didn't seem to notice him; they were obviously showing off for some girls sitting nearby.

"Yeah, it could be," Ned said, talking louder so Case could hear. His voice sounded doubtful, though. He sipped his milk and glanced cautiously at his food; Ned was always careful to make his milk last until all his food was gone. "Well, it might work," he added. "If someone actually comes in to help Granny on Thursdays."

"When'll you find out?"

Ned shrugged and bit off a corner of his sandwich. He pushed his glasses farther up his nose. "Who knows? Sometimes they move fast, sometimes they move slow. If it's an emergency, they move fast."

"But this isn't an emergency," Case said with a relieved sigh.

"Excuse me," a soft voice said behind them. The boys turned around: it was Ellie Lane, Case's friend from English class. She was quiet and graceful, thin and tall, with long, shiny brown hair. She reminded Case of an antelope. "Hi, Casey," she said, serious as usual. "Hi, Ned," she added with a smile.

"You guys know each other?" Case asked, surprised.

"We have math together. Last period," Ned explained.

Ellie smoothed back her hair and held it behind her neck in a temporary ponytail; then she let it fall onto her turquoise sweater. "Ned, are you really going to join the chess club? Mr. Branowski told me you might."

Ned nodded, gulping the rest of his sandwich. His broken glasses slid back down his nose, but Ellie didn't seem to notice. "Why? Are you?" Ned finally asked.

"Maybe," Ellie said. "You're supposed to sign up in the counselor's office. I was thinking about going over there now. Want to come?"

"Sure," Ned said, pushing his chair back. He wadded up his lunch sack, ignoring the lumps made by his uneaten apple and the leftover chocolate chip cookies Mrs. Hill had made. He

stood up abruptly. "Let me just throw this stuff away. You want the rest of my milk, Case?"

Staring at them, Case quickly nodded and reached for the milk. "Yeah. Yeah, sure. Okay. Thanks," he added, but Ned and Ellie were already halfway across the big steamy room.

*Ned—goofy, clumsy Ned—he knows Ellie?* Case turned to stare at Ned's half-empty milk carton, amazed, and not at all pleased. It felt weird having his separate friends make friends with each other—and then go off without him.

# 6

## MYSTERIOUS

*"Um, this is Ellie Lane, calling for Casey. Casey, I just need to get Ned Ryan's phone number, to tell him something about chess club. Can you call me back tonight? Thanks."*

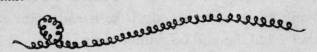

"Who's Ellie Lane?" Lily asked, frowning with suspicion.

"She's this girl in English," Case said, his voice low. Their mother was putting away groceries, but Case was sure she could hear their conversation.

"Is she pretty?"

"I don't know," Case said, annoyed. He didn't want to talk about Ellie. "She's okay, I guess. Why are you asking all these questions?"

"Well, how'd she get our phone number?" Lily continued, relentless.

"I guess I gave it to her. We were working together on the class newspaper last semester," Case said. "Lily, don't you have something to *do*?"

Lily thought this over. "No," she said, settling back into the big chair next to the telephone as though her favorite TV show were about to start. When Case hesitated, she said, "Well? Aren't you going to call her?"

"I will, I will. After dinner."

"But she's waiting now," Lily insisted. "She wants to talk to Ned."

"I know, I know," Case shouted. "You don't have to keep saying it! I'll call her when I'm ready, okay? It's no big deal!" He stomped across the floor to his alcove and yanked the striped curtains shut tight behind him.

"I only said it once," Lily remarked to her mother's back. "He's the one saying everything twice."

"I know, I know," Mrs. Hill said, echoing Case, as she turned around with a smile. "Don't worry about it, baby. Help me set the table."

*And leave me alone,* Case thought. *This is going to be weird enough.* He had sometimes daydreamed about calling Ellie—but he had never thought he'd be doing it to give her Ned's phone number!

"So how's it going?" Case asked Ned casually the next morning as they waited for the bus that would take them to school. He wanted to hear about Ellie's phone call. Above their heads, skinny tree branches seemed to shiver in the wind.

"You mean at home? With Granny? It's going pretty good," Ned said. "She's got one of those walkers for when she's alone in the house, and this lady comes to help her out sometimes. She takes her to the doctor and stuff. It's going—okay," he finished thoughtfully, pushing up his glasses with a free hand.

"Well, that's good. So you'll have time to join that chess club after school?"

"Huh? Oh, I guess," Ned said. "I'll give it a try. See who's good, and stuff."

*Like Ellie,* Case thought bitterly. Wasn't Ned even going to mention her call?

Ned peered down the wet street as a shiny flash of blue rounded the corner. *"Finally,"* he said. "Got your pass?"

The boys got on the bus and huddled together near the rear door. "Hey, how do the chess pieces move again?" Case asked, just for something to say.

"It's simple," Ned said patiently. "The king, he *looks* powerful, and he is, but he can only move one square, any direction, straight ahead or diagonal. The queen can move any direction too,

42

but she's the one who can just keep on going. The bishops move as far as they want, but it has to be on the diagonal. They just sort of slide on over, then pow! Knights can jump. They make sort of a hook move. They're the only ones who do that. They can be kind of sneaky. The rooks can go as far as they want in any direction, but it has to be in a straight line."

"They're the ones that look like castles?"

"Yeah. Sometimes they're *called* castles. They're pretty cool—there's this move where your rook can make sort of a fortress in the corner for your king. That's called 'castling.'"

"Castling," Case repeated automatically. It didn't even sound like a real word, somehow. Typical of chess, Case thought. No wonder the game always confused him.

"Why? You thinking of joining the club?" Ned asked.

"Me? I can't. I have to work at Mrs. Donovan's after school, remember?" Marge Donovan was a friend of the Hill family and had hired Case to do chores in her antique shop after school and on Saturdays. Case was glad to have an excuse not to join.

"Oh yeah, I forgot," Ned said.

"So who's in the club, anyway, besides you and Ellie?"

"Mostly older kids. I may get some good games," Ned said happily. Then he added, "Oh, jeez."

An old man had entered the bus and was shouting at the driver. "I ride free!" he said, his voice rumbling, almost out of control. "I showed you my pass. I worked for forty-two years, I ride free!"

"Not at rush hour," the driver kept repeating. Everyone on the bus was either watching the two men or staring fixedly out the window; the bus didn't move an inch.

"Forty-two years! I ride free!"

"Rush hour. Pay the fare."

"Great," Ned whispered. "Stalemate. More chess—I'll tell you about it later."

"I have a feeling it means we're going to be late," Case whispered back.

"Looks that way."

Case hurried to homeroom, still not quite believing Ned hadn't told him Ellie had called last night. Ms. Riley was getting ready to take roll and read the day's bulletin.

*He didn't even mention it,* Case thought as he slid

44

into his seat, just in time. *It's not like I expect him to tell me everything. It's not like I even care! But Ned keeps saying what great friends we are, and now it's like he's hiding something from me.* He didn't know who he was madder at—Ellie, for turning things upside down, or Ned, for keeping secrets.

Ms. Riley perched uneasily on the edge of her desk and eyed her homeroom class over the top of the announcement sheet, a smudge of chalk dust decorating one sleeve of her sweater. Her long, horsey face looked suspicious, as usual. It was as though she was expecting people to make fun of her, Case thought.

Today, she seemed to be searching her students' faces for something that would prove her worst suspicions about them true. She cleared her throat and got ready to read.

"Ms. Riley?" a voice asked from the back of the room.

"Yes, Tyler?" Ms. Riley looked up and smiled a little. She seemed to like Tyler, but Case couldn't figure out why. Tyler was one of the most popular kids in sixth grade, and he liked to show off to his friends in homeroom, often at Ms. Riley's expense.

"Is it true they're not going to have daylight savings time this year?" Tyler was asking.

A few girls giggled, and Ms. Riley scowled. "No daylight savings time? Where did you hear that?"

"Some kids. I heard that Philadelphia decided it was too much trouble, turning back all those clocks. I figured you'd know for sure."

"I think you turn the clocks *forward* in the spring," Ms. Riley said, looking flustered. "Isn't it 'Spring forward, fall back'?"

Case started to feel a little sorry for her. The bulletin drooped against her desk.

First-period buzzer rang, and the homeroom kids jumped up and swarmed toward the door. Tyler had won! He'd distracted Ms. Riley just long enough to mess up attendance and announcements.

"Way to go," a couple of boys laughed to Tyler as they shouldered their way out. It was said just loud enough for Ms. Riley to hear.

Case looked back at her face then, and their eyes met. "Well, what are you waiting for?" she asked. "Leave!"

*Hey, don't take it out on me,* Case thought angrily, but he went.

In English class, Ellie Lane was settling neatly

back into her chair when Case entered the room. She whispered something to Bryan DeLillo, who had the seat behind Case, and she smiled at Case as he sat down. "Thanks for calling me last night," she said. Behind him, Case felt Bryan stir with excitement: Bryan was shy, but he was becoming a famous school gossip.

"Relax, Bry," Case said over his shoulder. "I was giving her someone else's phone number."

"Yeah? Whose?" Bryan whispered urgently.

"This guy I know. It wasn't anything personal, don't get your hopes up." Bryan gave him a little shove between his shoulder blades as Ms. Yardley—Case's favorite teacher—started to speak.

Beside him, Ellie smiled a mysterious little smile, and suddenly Case felt like a fool—but he couldn't figure out why. He knew he didn't like the feeling, though.

# 7

## FAMILY

"Hey, Case! Come on down after dinner, if you can. I need to talk to you about something. Won't take long, pal. Call me back if you can't make it. Otherwise, see you! Oh—this is Buddy, by the way."

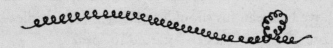

"I knew it was Buddy!" Lily shouted in triumph. "I already guessed, even before he said it."

"You're a good guesser, baby," Mrs. Hill said.

"I better go talk to him now," Case said. "It might be important."

His mother thought, then shrugged. "I guess that's okay. As long as you leave enough time for your homework."

"Can I go too?" Lily asked. "I want to go to Buddy's. Champion *misses* me."

"I'm sure he does, Lily, but Buddy asked for Case. It sounds like he wants to talk business."

"You think I can't talk business," Lily said, frowning. Case could tell she was about to lose her temper.

"No, I don't think that," Case said, trying to come up with an idea—fast—to calm his little sister. "I'll tell Buddy you need some business too, just for you. Okay?"

"Really?" Lily said, clutching Case's arm. "Do you think I can do it?"

"You don't even know what the business *is* yet, Lily," her mother said, laughing.

"But Casey thinks I can do it," Lily repeated, serious.

Case remembered the day he and their landlord Buddy had become friends the previous summer. It was when Buddy had first talked about his accident. They'd been in the park, with Champion.

"So when are you going to ask me about the chair?" Buddy had asked.

"The chair?" Case said, not sure what Buddy meant.

"Come on, Case, the chair. My wheelchair. When are you going to ask me about it?"

 49

"Now, I guess," Case said slowly. But no words followed.

"Well, why do you think I'm in it?" Buddy prompted him.

"Because you can't walk."

"Right. And why do you think I can't walk?"

"Maybe you were in a war?" Case guessed. It was what he had been thinking all along, really. He wasn't sure what war it could have been, but he had imagined the battle many times. It was kind of exciting to think about war, but he didn't like to think about Buddy getting hurt.

"Nope, no war, Case." There was a long silence. Champion snapped at a fly without even opening his eyes. "You disappointed?" Buddy asked.

"Of course not!" Case said, but he was, a little. That made him feel even worse. He hurried on. "Maybe you were born that way? This kid in my old school was. He was in a wheelchair too."

"No, I wasn't born this way."

"What happened, then?"

"I was in a motorcycle accident, Case, when I was nineteen."

"How old are you now?" Case asked. He could never tell with grownups. They all looked kind of old to him.

"I'm thirty-eight. That means I've been in this chair half my life—so far. Want to hear about the accident?"

"I guess." Did he really? Case wasn't sure, but he didn't want to say no.

"It was raining that night, so I was being extra careful. I was wearing a helmet and everything."

"Were you drunk?"

"No way. The woman who hit me sure was, but she was in a big old car, so she never got a scratch on her."

"But that's not fair!"

Buddy looked at him and smiled a crooked smile. "I guess not, but it happened."

"Did they put her in jail?"

"For a little while. Just overnight. Part of one night, really."

"She didn't go to jail, when she could have killed you? I can't believe it. Was she sorry at least?"

"I don't know—I never saw her after the trial. Who cares? Probably she was, maybe she was. What difference would it make?"

"But couldn't the doctors fix it so you could walk again?"

Buddy shook his head. "No. They did what they could."

"But doctors can do anything now," Case said angrily.

"They can do a lot, but some things they can't fix."

"Are you sure? Maybe there's something they didn't try. Or something new."

"I'm *sure,* Case. Believe me."

"But what did you do then? After the accident?"

"I got used to it. I went ahead with the rest of my life. I can still do a lot of things, you know, Case. I went back to school and tried to figure out how to make a living."

"Everything changed for you, in just a second," Case said.

"Yeah," Buddy agreed. "It was hard knowing I could never hike the Appalachian Trail or learn to play tennis any better. Hey, I can't even walk upstairs anymore. And I have to plan every move in advance now. That's almost the worst. I used to like surprises."

Case had looked at the grass under his sneakers and felt hot tears fill his eyes. But he didn't cry. He didn't want Buddy to think he was soft. "It's not right!" he finally said.

"What's not right?"

"That someone can do one wrong thing, and

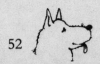

you're the one who has to pay. And what that lady did hurt other people, too, not just you. Like your family, probably."

"Yeah, it hurt my family plenty."

"And it's not fair that another person can make one wrong choice," Case went on, "like turning a corner too fast or deciding to rob a truck, and then wham! Your whole life is over. It's not right! And what about you?" Case persisted. "You weren't doing anything wrong. That lady hit *you*. It's not fair," he repeated.

"No, but it's the way things work out sometimes. And you can't change what's already happened. You could drive yourself crazy even thinking about it."

"Well, it stinks," Case said. Champion stood up then and stretched. He made a squeaking sound as he yawned. Buddy and Case started laughing, and Champion looked at them and wagged his tail. Case felt a tear spill over and creep down one cheek.

"Come on, Case," Buddy had said, "let's head back home. We don't want your mom to worry."

"So what job do you think Lily could do?" Buddy asked Case, wheeling his chair across the

53

shiny wood floor. He turned up the temperature on the thermostat a little, and a radiator pinged.

"Maybe she could lick some letters shut? And put on stamps? That could be her job. Mom lets her do that sometimes," Case said, settling back into one of Buddy's sleek leather chairs. He liked Buddy's apartment—it was so *modern*. No frills, nothing old and battered. No traces of some sad old life. Case wanted to live like that someday.

Buddy frowned as he wheeled over to the refrigerator. "Cider?" he asked, and Case nodded. "Well," Buddy said, considering aloud, "she'd need someone to watch her do that. I need to think up something she can do alone."

"She can mess things up for you!" Case joked.

"Lily's not *that* bad, but you may be onto something. How good is she at throwing things away?"

Case looked at him, a question in his eyes.

"My old pages," Buddy said. Buddy was a writer and used up a lot of paper. "Lily could be my personal paper shredder!"

"You'd pay her to do that?"

"Sure, a little. Like a penny a page?"

"Lily would *love* that. She thinks pennies are the best. In fact, if she tears up twenty sheets of paper, you'd better not give her two dimes."

54

"Thanks for the warning. Hey, I have to let you get back to your homework, pal. Here's the deal. I have to go away for a while, to visit my sister in Cape May."

"When?"

"Starting a week from Saturday. I'll get back the Saturday after that, the day before Easter. But there's a hitch—she's allergic to dogs." Champion groaned in his sleep and stretched out his legs with a quiver. "My feelings exactly, Champ!" Buddy said with a laugh. "Anyway, he'd be miserable there. She's got so many little china doodads in every room, Champion would have to tiptoe through on his hind legs. It's hard enough with this," he added, patting his wheelchair like a cowboy patting a loyal old horse.

"But why go, then?" Case asked, confused. "I mean, it's none of my business, but..."

"She's my sister, Case. The only family I've got left. Besides, I like her."

Case tried to picture himself as a grownup going to visit a cranky old Lily who collected a lot of stuff—little dolls and doll clothes, maybe—and hated dogs. *But Lily will never hate dogs,* he thought with a grin. "So where will Champion be staying?" he asked Buddy. "Here?"

55

Buddy nodded. "There's a kennel way out of town, but Champion doesn't like it. I wasn't too pleased with the way he looked last time I picked him up there, either. They hadn't been brushing him regularly. I'm not ruling it out, though, Case. Just tell me if you don't think you can manage—I know you're busy."

"What would I have to do?"

"Feed and walk him in the morning and right away when you get home, and maybe bring him up to your apartment for a couple of hours every night. He'll be lonely."

Case grinned. "Not once Lily gets her hands on him, he won't. It sounds great." He gazed at the sleeping dog and imagined doing his homework upstairs with the Akita curled up next to him.

"Maybe you could brush him at night. Or Lily could, if she wants to."

"Knowing her, she'll want to. She can spend an hour just fixing her doll's hair. Imagine what she could do with big old Champion!" They looked over at the dog. Case pictured tiny plastic barrettes clipped into his thick fur. Champion gave another groan in his sleep.

"Well, talk it over with your mom," Buddy said. "See what she thinks. This involves her, too, if

Champion goes up there for nightly visits."

"Okay, but I'm sure she'll say yes."

"I'll talk to her in a couple of days about what to pay you."

"You don't have to pay me," Case said. "I mean, you already pay me enough to take Champion out running." Case and Buddy had worked out an informal exercise schedule so the dog would get at least three runs a week with Case in addition to his daily walks with Buddy.

"No, I'll feel better about it if I pay you. Otherwise it'll have to be the kennel."

"Okay, then," Case said, feeling uncomfortable. He hated talking about money; it made him think of his father. His dad had always been obsessed with what things cost, with how much everyone else had, and so on. "But don't forget," Case added, "I wanted to do some extra work to pay you back for the answering machine."

"Noted," Buddy said. "Now," he continued, "I've got another question for you."

"What?"

"How's your dad doing? I haven't heard you or Lily talk much about him lately."

Case lifted a shoulder and looked away. "He's all right, I guess." Thinking about his father made him think about their old life in Cherry Hill, New Jersey. Only half an hour—and a million years—away.

"He doesn't call us much anymore," Case continued. "Just our answering machine, if he wants Mom to send him something. He loves that machine. It's the perfect invention for him. He can tell us all what to do without actually talking with us. He can call when he knows we're out, since it's not long distance," Case added bitterly. "Otherwise they have to call collect." He pictured his father using the prison pay phone at Southwark Penitentiary, where he was serving time for armed robbery, and he grew silent.

"So you're not visiting him much?"

"Only on holidays. *Big* holidays. He told Mom the visits were too hard on him." The penitentiary was right there in Philadelphia, but Dennis Hill had only let them visit three times so far, at the end of summer, at Thanksgiving, and at Christmas.

"What does Lily have to say about all this?" Lily was her father's favorite and had taken his imprisonment the hardest of any of them.

"She doesn't talk about it much. I think she's still busy trying to figure out whose fault it all is. I mean, nothing can be Dad's fault, according to

Lily, and she knows it isn't *her* fault, because she loves him so much. That leaves me and Mom. Mostly me."

"So it's your fault your dad doesn't want to see anyone?"

"Guess so!" Case said with a self-mocking grin. "But mostly she doesn't talk about it."

"That's rough. So are you folks going for an Easter visit?"

"Yeah, probably. That's a big enough holiday." Case wanted to groan, just like Champion. "Our Christmas visit was a disaster. He and my mom had this huge fight, and Lily threw up all over the place." *And there were hardly any presents, and we all had to act like nothing was the matter,* he added to himself.

"But Dad's already left a couple of messages about what to bring on Easter," Case continued. "He says he wants ham. It drives my mom crazy. Lily likes hearing his voice, though, even if he doesn't say anything much. But then he always says, 'A special hug for my Lily-baby,' at the end, so that's good enough for her."

"Poor Lily."

"Yeah. Well, I guess it's better than nothing. For her anyway," Case added.

Later, lying in bed, Case thought about his father some more. How could he have robbed that truck? Apart from everything else, didn't he know what it would do to his family? It was like throwing them away!

What was his father doing—right now? *I bet he's not thinking about us anyway,* Case thought, bitter. *Why start now?* He pulled the covers up under his chin, smoothed them down perfectly straight, and stared up at the ceiling, frowning.

Case remembered that he had just turned five when his father first got in trouble. Maybe trouble had happened even before then, but the day after Case's fifth birthday, the doorbell rang. Case opened the door, and there stood two policemen. One frowned down at him and asked, "Your daddy home, little boy?" Case carefully shut the door and walked into the kitchen.

His mother was patting a meat loaf. "Who was at the door, Case?"

"Men."

"What do you mean, men? Where are they?"

"Outside."

"Casey!" She quickly rinsed her hands and

rushed out of the kitchen. Case sat under the kitchen table, slid his birthday present from his pocket—a tiny electronic game his father had given him—and played until his mother finally told him dinner was ready.

Dinner was late that night. Case couldn't remember if his father ate with them, but he did remember how his dad had yelled at his mom later, and at Case, too. And it wasn't their fault!

Lily hadn't even been born yet.

There had been other bad times, too, Case remembered, and lots of fighting. Then the fighting stopped. Sometimes his dad hadn't been around much, but most of the time everything seemed normal. There was no crying then, no fighting, no bad words, nothing. Not even much talking. *Just a normal family like other families, doing regular stuff.*

*I was still eleven when the big trouble started,* he thought, throwing a pillow onto the floor. It had been a little more than twelve months ago. Only a year, but it seemed like ancient history. History, Case thought. He tried telling it to himself, like a bedtime story:

Chapter One. Once upon a time, something happened to our family.

Lily was still really little then. I was walking her home from a friend's house, when I saw Mom backing the car out of the driveway. She looked like she was crying, and I was scared. Lily didn't see her face. Mom saw us, and she rolled down the window. She said, "I'll be back. I left you a note. Stay inside, and don't answer the phone or open the door. There's cereal if you get hungry, but don't use the stove." I remember I just stared at her.

Lily said, "Mommy? Can I come with you?" She tried to pull her hand away from my hand.

Mom said, "No, baby. Stay with Case. Go on inside, Case. Everything will be all right."

I pulled Lily into the house as Mom drove away. I locked the front door behind us, then put on the chain. Lily finally yanked her hand away from mine and sat down hard on the hall floor. She said, "I hate you." She blamed me! I remember I turned on the TV for her and told her I'd fix her lunch. Cereal.

She said, "Cereal is for breakfast, stupid." She was crying.

The phone rang a lot that afternoon, but I didn't answer it. I wouldn't let Lily answer it either. I told her, "We're not home."

She said, "Where are we, then?" I said I didn't know.

Mom came back just when I was trying to figure out what to feed Lily next. She walked in the back door and put her purse on the kitchen counter like nothing was wrong. She looked funny, though. She said, "It all looks just the same."

I said, "What does?"

She said, "The yard, the house. But everything has changed."

I was scared. I told her, "Everything's the same, Mom."

She said, "Okay, Casey, everything's the same. Nothing has changed, and it never will." I wonder if she even remembers saying that. Did she know it wasn't true when she said it? She must have...Did she lie on purpose, or couldn't she help it?

Case tried to untangle his covers. The sheet had gotten twisted around one leg, and the quilt had come untucked at the bottom. He muffled a yelp of frustration as he tried to kick everything straight.

Chapter Two. I remember the second time Dad's picture was in the newspaper. It was the day after the trial ended. I saw it in the school library. So did everyone, probably. I know Paul and Tony did. Tony's mouth was probably watering, my so-called friend. He reminds me a little of Bryan DeLillo. Anyway, he just had to be the big expert on the trial. He told other kids stuff I told him in secret. Jeremy had already moved away by then.

I kept waiting for Mom to say something about the trial. She never did. I know she was in court for it, though.

It was a long trial, almost a week. Paul wouldn't talk to me much—his mother told him not to. He said, "We're still friends and everything, but we can't hang out until it's over." I guess he meant until the judge said Dad was innocent, but she never did.

When I got home from school each day, Lily was there with a babysitter, not with Mom. Mom came home in time for dinner each night, but she didn't eat much. She gave Lily a bath and asked me about my homework. I could have said anything, she wasn't listening. Then she went to bed right after we did.

I would lie there awake and stare at the ceiling. I knew that pretty soon it would all be over.

But I never thought things could change so fast. One day there was a sign in our front yard saying our house was for sale. Lily was excited by the sign at first, but I knew what it meant. We had to keep the house picked up all the time. Instead, I felt like setting booby traps for the strangers who went snooping through our rooms, even our closets.

Once Lily figured out we were moving, she got mad. She said, "How can Daddy find us if we move?" I told Mom it was Dad's house too. She said it wasn't, that Grandmama and Grandpa Jake had given her the house before they died. It was her house, and she could sell it if she wanted. She said we needed the money to make a new start. She promised she would tell Dad where we were going.

Chapter Three. Lily cheered up when she heard we were moving to Philadelphia. I guess she thought we'd be closer to Dad, since he's in Southwark Penitentiary. That's in Philadelphia too, but it's not the reason we moved here. Mom said it would be easier to get a job in the city, and she could sell her car.

Philadelphia isn't that far from Cherry Hill, even though they're in different states, but they're really a whole world apart.

Sometimes I want to yell at Mom and say, "You promised nothing would change. You liar! Isn't lying to your kids a crime too? Isn't that at least as bad as trying to steal some stupid VCRs?" But most of the time, I'm glad we moved so fast. Most of the time...

His thoughts drifted sleepily to Ned. Ned had never even known his father, not ever! What would that be like? Maybe Ned was the lucky one. Wouldn't not knowing your father be better than having a dad who was in jail?

Case imagined someone playing chess somewhere with a tall, skinny, serious man whose

glasses kept sliding down his nose. Ned's father! *You lose,* Case imagined himself saying to the man. *You lose, big.*

*And you do too, Dad.*

# 8

## ALMOST SPRING

"It's me. I want to say about the ham, make sure it's spiral-sliced, not one of those canned jobs. And wear the red dress, you know the one. Case, what's happening? I heard you got a C in math. Shape up. Don't forget, you still answer to me. Which reminds me, are you doing any sports yet? Because you should. A special hug for my Lily-baby! Ask your Mama to make me some of that chocolate cake of hers for Easter. We'll have us a party!"

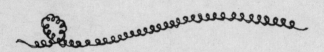

"Can we play it again?" Lily begged, bouncing up and down in the big chair.

"Lily, you heard it three times already," Mrs. Hill said as she tossed the salad. "Dinner is almost ready, baby—go wash up."

"How about if I just listen to the part about the chocolate cake and the hug?"

"I'll show you how to work the buttons. You can play it yourself."

"Or save it. Maybe we could save it?"

"Oh, definitely," Case said from across the room. "I wouldn't want to miss hearing Dad say what a dummy I am in math all the time."

"He doesn't say it *all* the time. And anyway, he probably just doesn't want you to be a dummy, Case," Lily pointed out. "That shouldn't make you mad."

"Well, it does. And how come he thinks I have to answer to him? He's not even here. It's not fair anyway—I can't ever call him back and tell him to mind his own business! He doesn't have an answering machine. Lucky him."

"No wonder Daddy is so mad at us," Lily said. "No wonder! I—"

"Lily," Mrs. Hill interrupted, "you can listen to the message two more times, with the volume down. After that, it's over until the next phone call. Understood?"

Something in her mother's voice made Lily nod quietly in agreement, and—except for the deep rumble of Dennis Hill's words—the room was quiet until they sat down for dinner.

"So what's new?" Case asked Ned the next morning on their way to school.

Ned shifted the weight of his backpack from one bony shoulder to another. A little stuffing poked out of a rip in his jacket, Case noticed. "Where?" Ned finally said. "At home, or at school?"

"Home, I meant. My mom was asking me," Case explained. "She wants to know if it's time for another cleanup party."

"No, we're okay," Ned said. He looked worried, though.

"All right, I'll tell her," Case said, uncertain how much more to ask.

Ned hesitated, then spoke again. "I mean, we're okay about the cleaning, but it would be good if your mom wanted to bring some more food over."

"Fried chicken, maybe," Case said, remembering the living room picnic they had shared.

"Granny wouldn't do so great with that these days," Ned said slowly.

"What do you mean?"

"She's been kind of wobbly lately. Sometimes she feels sick. So maybe rice pudding or something? Your mom made that once when I was over. Granny could eat that, I bet." Ned's face was serious as he pushed his sliding glasses up higher.

"How long has she been so sick?"

"I didn't say she was sick, just woozy," Ned explained. "She says it's probably spring fever."

"But it's still pretty cold out," Case said doubtfully, looking through a steamy bus window to what dull gray sky he could see. "I don't think it's even spring yet."

"Well, it's almost spring. Maybe Granny just means she's sick of winter!" Ned said. "She's been inside the house a long time. Or maybe she needs more vitamins. She hasn't been eating very much."

"What about that lady from the city? What does she say?"

"Granny doesn't tell her everything," Ned said reluctantly. "She says we have to keep some things to ourselves."

"Well, you get vitamin D from the sun, I think," Case said, to change the subject. "Maybe she just needs some extra vitamin D?"

"Ask your mom," Ned said. "And say something about the rice pudding," he added, repeating, "I *know* Granny could eat that."

"Casey," Marge Donovan said after school that day, "what do you think about doing an Easter window this year?"

Case was polishing one of the many little silver

71

sports trophy cups that filled a display cabinet in Treasure Trove, the antique shop on Third Street, where he worked after school and on Saturdays.

He had just finished stomping flat a big pile of cardboard cartons for recycling and was seated at a small table with Mrs. Donovan. He rinsed a tennis trophy in a plastic basin of warm water. His fingers were getting puckery. "You mean like bunnies and stuff?" he asked doubtfully, trying to remember if there were any Easter things in the shop.

"Oh, everyone does bunnies and chocolate Easter eggs," Mrs. Donovan said. "Maybe you could come up with something different. It doesn't even have to be Easter, as a matter of fact. It could be about spring. But people have been asking when we're going to have another Casey window." Since the school year had begun, Case had done three funny window displays for Mrs. Donovan's shop, one for Halloween, one for Christmas, and one for Valentine's Day.

"You want me to use some of Lily's stuffed animals again?" he asked.

Mrs. Donovan laughed. "If they fit in with your plan, and *if* you get permission from Lily. Mr. Fluff *has* become quite a favorite of a few customers!" she hinted. Lily's much-loved plush cat had starred in two displays so far. He'd been especially effective as the angel at the top of the shop's big Christmas tree.

"When do you want the window finished?" Case asked.

"Let's see—this is Monday, and Easter is a week from next Sunday. Think you can install the display by Saturday?"

"Yeah, okay," Case said, thinking hard. He reached automatically for another silver cup and started polishing as his eyes scanned the crowded shop, looking for things he could use in the display. His fingers brushed the cup's dented surface. Faint engraved letters spelled out the name of a long-ago winner, someone who had been good at sports. But the letters had almost faded away, so many springs had passed since then.

*Well, at least there are some things I'm good at,* Case thought, *even if Dad doesn't think they count for much.*

*Hey,* he thought suddenly, *I have an idea! Way back in the corner of the storeroom—I think there's something perfect for the Easter window...*

# 9
# SOMEPLACE LIKE HOME

"Hello? Hello? Is anyone there? It's Hazel Ryan. I think I may need some help. Something's wrong, I feel so dizzy. Neddy's at school, and I don't know who to call. I'm not sure about an ambulance, and my helper's not coming in today. I'll try to find your work number. I know you gave it to me. I'll call you there. Well—goodbye."

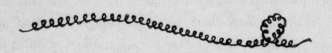

Mrs. Hill, Case, and Lily huddled in a little circle around the answering machine, listening to Ned's Granny. "Is she dead, Mama?" Lily asked.

"No, baby. But by the time I got over there, she was unconscious."

"Did you remember to dial nine-one-one?" Lily asked. Her mother nodded.

Case swallowed hard; his throat felt like there was something caught in it. "Is she in the hospital?" he managed to ask.

His mother nodded again. "I rode with her in the ambulance. They roused her a little."

"She woke up?" Lily asked.

"Enough to worry about Ned. We called a social worker when we got to the hospital, and Hazel signed something called a Voluntary Placement Order for Ned. The doctors started her on fluids, and they're hoping she'll be all right. It will take some time to find out, though."

"But what's wrong with her?" Case asked. "I thought that city lady was taking care of everything."

"People still get sick sometimes, Case, even if you watch them every minute. Ned's Granny hasn't been well for a long time, remember."

"But when will she come home?" Case persisted.

"I don't know," Mrs. Hill said. "Not for a while anyway. And Case, she might not ever come home."

"Wait a minute—who's taking care of Ned?" he

asked suddenly, imagining his friend returning home from school to an empty house. "Where's Ned?"

"Ned's fine, Case. The social worker went right over to school from the hospital. They called Ned out of class and explained the situation. Then they took him to his house, so Ned could pick up some clothes and so forth."

"But where is he?" Case repeated.

"He's in foster care for a while, until Human Services can straighten things out. And Lacy is with their neighbor, who's crazy about her, so don't worry about that."

"That's good, but what's foster care?" Lily asked, looking as scared as Case felt.

"That's where someone else takes care of children when they need it," her mother explained.

"You mean like an *orphanage*?" Lily asked, horrified.

"No, baby. It's a family who's appointed to take care of kids when it's necessary. Just until things get straightened out," she repeated.

"But *we're* a family," Case objected. "Why can't *we* take care of Ned?"

"We don't have room, for one thing."

"He sleeps over sometimes. There's room then, isn't there?"

"Human Services wants Ned to be someplace like home, Case. As close as possible anyway. They want Ned to have his own bed, and desk, and so on."

"But what about school?" Case asked.

"Maybe Ned gets to go on vacation," Lily said. "Because he's so sad."

"He won't miss any school," her mother said. "The social worker found a foster home for Ned near Ben Franklin. She said that's a miracle, practically. So Ned's lucky, he won't even have to change schools. His life will be as normal as possible, until—"

"Until his Granny dies," Lily said, matter-of-fact.

"Shut up!" Case shouted.

"Casey, calm down. And Lily, you don't have to say every little thing that pops into your head."

"I don't," Lily said.

"Mom," Case interrupted, "what's going to happen to him?"

"I guess one of several things," his mother said reluctantly. "He could stay in foster care until

77

Mrs. Ryan gets better. Then he could move back home with her."

"But you don't think that's going to happen," Case said, blunt.

"No. No, I don't. Another thing that might happen is Ned could return to Texas and live with his mother again. They'll be trying to locate her to see if that's a possibility."

"What about his daddy?" Lily asked. "Ned could move in with his daddy, and they could play checkers together!"

"It's chess, and Ned doesn't even know where his father is," Case said. "He never did."

"That's just dumb, Case. How could you not know where your daddy is? We know where ours is."

*Yeah, in jail,* Case thought, bitter. He turned back to his mother. "What if they can't find Ned's mother? Or what if she doesn't want him?"

"That's even dumber," Lily said angrily. "Who wouldn't want Ned?"

"Well, we don't, I guess," Case said, shooting a dirty look at his mother.

"Casey, that's not fair," she said. "Human Services doesn't just hand children out like stray

puppies. We don't get to decide about Ned. There'll be a hearing in a couple of days to figure out what will be happening to him."

"So other people will move him around, just like in chess," Case said darkly. "Anyway, he's *not* lucky."

"And how come you keep calling him a child?" Lily asked. "He's the same age as Case."

"In the eyes of the law, he's still a dependent child."

"And now he's living with a strange family," Case said. "Can we go see him, at least? Or call him?"

"I don't know yet exactly where he is, Case," his mother said gently. "You can talk to him tomorrow, though, at school. Get his new phone number. Maybe even go over and see where he's living."

"I want to talk to him tonight," Case said, stubborn.

"Well, maybe he'll call here," his mother said, trying to reassure him.

But the telephone was silent. It was an unusually quiet night.

# 10

## DIVIDED-BY

"Hey, Case, it's Buddy. Don't know if I'll see you before I go, but don't forget I'm leaving the day after tomorrow for Cape May. I put my key in your mailbox, and I'm leaving my sister's number—and the vet's—on the kitchen table. Champion's kibble is shut in the bathroom, and his leash will be by the front door. Thanks, pal!"

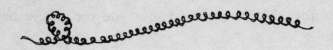

It was Thursday night, and Case listened to Buddy's message as he touched the note from Ned that lay nestled deep in his pocket. The note's folded edges felt soft against Case's fingertips, and he knew what it said by heart; he had read it at least a dozen times. Mr. Petroni had given the note to Case after school when Case stopped by the candy stand to say hello. The stand was right next to the bus stop, and Case always said hi, even if he didn't have money for a snack that day.

"That nice boy Ned left this note for you, Casey," Mr. Petroni had said.

"He did? When?"

"Early, after lunch. He was with this lady, but he kind of sneaked it into my hand. A secret spy message, huh?"

"Yeah, kind of," Case had said, reaching for the note. He read it on the bus:

> Case—I'm going home early this after-noon, well, not home, but you know. I said I'm sick, but not really. Don't call me there. I NEED YOUR HELP, can't explain yet. Meet me tomorrow R.T. at 4, bring $$. I'll pay you back, I promise. PRIVATE!! Ned

"Case? Casey?" his mother was saying.

"He can't hear you. I hypnotized him," Lily said, smug. She had seen Bugs Bunny being hypnotized in a cartoon the Saturday before, and she'd been practicing ever since.

"I *can* hear you," Case said. "But what did you say?"

"I asked if you need to talk with Buddy before he leaves for his sister's."

Case shook his head. "Nope."

"Maybe we should bring Champion up here tonight, just for practice," Lily said.

"I think we can wait, baby," Mrs. Hill said. "I'm going to start dinner. Case, you go put all the dirty clothes and towels in the big plastic laundry basket. Lily, you empty all the wastebaskets into this trash bag."

"What about my homework?" Lily objected.

Case laughed a little. "You have homework now? In first grade?"

"Sure," Lily said, indignant. "Worse than yours, I bet. Divided-bys and everything."

"You don't have division in first grade," Case said.

"We start it next week," Lily informed him loftily.

"Well, all the chores divided by all the available Hills equals one happy family," Mrs. Hill said, pulling a sack of carrots out of the refrigerator.

"You can't divide people up," Lily said as she fumbled with the big plastic bag, trying to open it. She corrected herself: "You can divide up families, though, I guess."

"What do you mean?"

"Like that judge did with us and Daddy," Lily explained.

*And Ned's not much better off,* Case thought as he carried an armload of dirty clothes to the waiting basket. *First his father left, then he was taken away from his mother, and now he's losing his Granny.* Little red and blue socks dropped behind Case like tiny footprints.

"Hey! Be careful, Case," Lily scolded him. "Those are my lucky socks."

"All of them?" Case asked.

"Yeah, what's wrong with that?"

"Nothing," Case said, thinking of Ned again. "I guess luck is one thing I *do* believe in. Bad luck, anyway."

Right before lunch the next day, Case called Marge Donovan at the antique shop from the pay phone near the school office. "Mrs. Donovan? Hi, it's me."

"Casey! Is anything wrong? Where are you?"

"I'm at school, and everything's fine. But—um, I can't come there this afternoon."

"Why, are you sick? Do you need someone to come get you?"

Case had never missed a day of work before. He kicked at the wall beneath the phone and said, "No, I'm fine. And don't worry, I'll finish the display window tomorrow morning. I have it all planned out."

"Okay, Casey." There was a pause; then Mrs. Donovan asked, "Is everything all right at home, dear?"

"Oh, sure! I just have to—do some stuff this afternoon. For the display," he added suddenly. He started to kick the wall again, but a warning look from a passing teacher stopped his foot mid-air.

"If it's for work, then you're not really taking time off," Mrs. Donovan said. "You'll still get paid, Casey."

"That's okay," Case said, miserable. A tall girl glared at Case and jingled coins in her hand. "Uh, Mrs. Donovan? I have to go now. Someone else wants to use the phone."

"All right, dear. See you tomorrow, bright and early!"

"Okay," Case said, and he hung up.

Case chewed his chicken sandwich slowly, without tasting it. He stared across the crowded table, the usual cafeteria clatter surrounding him. It

was always loudest on Fridays. Bryan DeLillo sat next to him, chattering away about something— but Case had other things on his mind.

He could feel the thick wad of money he had shoved deep into his pants pocket: There was sixty-three dollars in tens, fives, and one-dollar bills. It was all he had saved since Christmas. He felt a tap on his shoulder and jumped.

"Don't choke to death," Ellie Lane said, laughing. Bryan laughed too and clutched at his throat, pretending to gag.

Case's eyes watered as he coughed. He grabbed his milk carton. "Hi," he finally gasped.

"Hi." Ellie slipped quietly into the seat next to his.

"Aren't you eating lunch today?" he asked her.

"I already finished."

"Want a cookie?" Case pushed a small bulging plastic bag in her direction. "Oatmeal. My mom made them."

"I'll take one," Bryan said with enthusiasm.

Ellie shrugged as if she didn't care, but she reached eagerly for a cookie. "Sure, I guess. Hey," she said after she had chewed and swallowed a neat curved bite, "is Ned okay?"

"Why?" Case's heart started to pound.

"He wasn't in math yesterday afternoon. I heard he went home sick. And he's not eating lunch with you today."

Case remembered sitting there the other day, when she'd walked away with Ned. He'd been left—sitting in this very chair, probably—with Ned's old milk carton in front of him. Ned hadn't told her anything about his Granny, he thought with satisfaction. Maybe he went and joined the chess club with Ellie, but Case was still the one he called when he was in trouble!

"Yeah," Bryan was saying. "I haven't seen him around lately either."

"Well, I'm kind of *worried* about him," Ellie said. Bryan's eyes glistened at this.

Next he would be blabbing it all around school, Case thought. This made him angry.

"So why don't you call Ned up, then, if you're so worried, and ask for yourself?" Case said to Ellie. "You have his phone number now."

"I did call him," Ellie said. She pushed her chair back and stood up. "I tried twice," she added. "No one answered, not even his Granny." Bryan was wriggling with excited interest.

Case shrugged, pretending to be bored. "Maybe they were out," he said. "They do lots of stuff

together, all the time. I guess he just hasn't told you."

When the final bell rang that Friday, Case walked quickly away from the usual bus stop and started toward Center City. His destination was "R.T."—Reading Terminal, the old train building that was now a popular tourist spot. Dozens of little shops lined the aisles inside the vast structure, and people browsed among snack bars looking for the perfect treat. Case and Ned had long ago found their favorite snack at the Amish pretzel stand: Aproned girls with pink cheeks and sheer white caps brushed butter on the freshly baked soft pretzels, wrapped them in waxy tissue, and handed them to waiting customers. Bottles of mustard stood nearby. Case's stomach growled noisily.

"Case!" an urgent voice called. Case looked around, but he couldn't see Ned anywhere. "Case," the voice repeated.

"Ned?"

"Here!" A boy sat at an unsteady little table next to an old man who seemed to be half asleep, crumbs on his vest. An oversize red Phillies cap covered the boy's hair, but the glasses wrapped with silver tape gave Ned away. He stood up quietly and gestured toward a vegetable stand nearby. "Shhh, don't say anything yet," Ned warned his friend. "Did anyone follow you?"

"No," Case said. "Why? Who would follow me?"

"Someone from Human Services, maybe. Some social worker. I ran away," he said, his voice low.

"From the foster home?"

"No, from the hearing. It was held this morning over on Vine Street."

"But why? What did they do?"

"Nothing—I didn't give them a chance. I ran away first, right before the hearing started. I said I had to use the bathroom, and then I ditched the social worker. It was real crowded."

Case looked around nervously. He didn't see anything suspicious, just a couple of men eating ice cream cones and a woman arguing with a fish seller. Her arms were loaded down with packages; some big kids ran by, jostling her, and she started to yell at them, too. "So the foster home was really terrible?" Case asked, sympathetic.

"The foster home?" Ned was surprised. "No, it was okay. There were two little kids there. Well, one's a baby, but Franklin, he's six. He's a pretty cool little guy, and Mrs. Juniper was nice. She's like the mom."

"I thought you didn't like little kids."

"Me too, but maybe it's just Lily. I mean, I *like* Lily and everything, she just makes me kind of nervous."

"I know what you mean, it's okay. What happened, though? Why did you run away?" Case asked as they started walking up and down the aisles—past the colorful vegetable displays, past the bakeries.

"I heard Mrs. Juniper on the phone Wednesday night, a few hours after I got there. I listened in." Case looked impressed, and Ned continued. "She was talking with the social worker. They're doing this big search for my mother, in Texas."

"But they already took you away from her once."

Ned's laugh was bitter. "I guess they want to give her another chance. Or they just want to dump me, so they don't have to worry about me."

"How could they find her, though? I thought even you didn't know where she was."

"I don't know exactly where. But the lady on the phone said they would do a search through the

 89

Department of Motor Vehicles, places like that. Pretty soon they'll find her." His thin shoulders sagged.

"Maybe that wouldn't be so bad, Ned. I mean, I'd miss you and everything if you had to move away, but maybe things have changed with your mom."

"That's just it. They *have* changed, but for the worse."

"How do you know?"

"I never told you, but a couple of years ago I found these letters my Granny got from her. Three letters, from Houston. She told Granny she had sort of like gotten married again, but the guy was really mean to her and the kids. She said she was trapped."

"More kids?" Ned nodded, glum. "Was she asking your Granny for help?"

"I couldn't tell. I don't think so. Granny doesn't have much extra money to help with."

"But if they find her..."

"They'll make me go live with her and her boyfriend, and everything will be worse for everybody, even for my mother. I'm scared to go, Case. I don't want to go!" Ned's voice broke over the last words. "My mom couldn't even manage when there was just her and me. That's okay—I liked living with Granny, once I got used to it. But why go dragging me back to Texas? Don't *I* get to say anything?"

"What do you want to do, though? Your Granny—"

"Granny's going into a nursing home, as soon as she gets well enough to leave the hospital. Her sister can't take care of her. She's even older than Granny. Mrs. Juniper was going to take me to the nursing home for visits. But I know they won't let me live with Granny anymore," Ned said, pausing to stare at some lobsters scuttling around in a tank. Their claws were banded; they piled onto one another like a litter of helpless kittens. "I liked the foster home pretty much, though," he added.

"You did?" Case couldn't get it out of his mind that he was helping to rescue Ned from foster care. He felt a little disappointed, somehow.

"Yeah, but I'm pretty sure they won't let me stay with Mrs. Juniper and Franklin and that baby what's-her-name if they find my mother. So I have to run away."

Case's hand found the wad of cash deep in his

pocket. "I brought money," he whispered, "but it's only sixty-three bucks. Where are you going to go?"

"I'm going to spend tonight in Philadelphia, in my old house. I still have the key. Then I have to leave—they'll find me too easy here."

"Won't they look for you in your old house tonight?"

"I'll keep the lights off, and I'll stay on the ground floor. That way I can get out the back if I have to. I don't think they have enough people to go searching for me, though. They probably don't even know I'm gone yet."

Case started thinking hard. Now was his chance to prove how much Ned needed him! "Look," he said, his voice growing more certain with each word, "I'm going over to your Granny's with you and make sure no one's poking around. You stay in the house, and I'll go buy you some food for dinner."

Ned looked relieved as he listened to his friend take charge. "Nothing I have to cook," he said.

"No," Case agreed. "Then you stay there all tomorrow morning, too, while I'm at work. If you have to bail out, I'll meet you in Headhouse Square, under the arch. Listen," he said suddenly, his mind working fast, "Buddy's leaving for vacation tomorrow morning."

"Yeah?" Ned said, his eyes lighting up.

"Yeah! I'll move you over to Buddy's at lunch, sneak you in. Mom will be at work, and Lily will still be at the sitter's, waiting for me to pick her up. I'll just go a little late. Buddy will be gone all week," Case added.

"A whole week," Ned said, relieved. "But won't he be mad?"

"I don't know," Case said. He didn't want to think about that—not now. "Your future is more important than him being mad, though."

"What about eating?" Ned asked.

"It'll have to be sandwiches and stuff, or you can cook while we're gone during the day, if you're careful. I'll get more food tomorrow. Champion will guard you. This will buy us some time anyway. Just don't run any water or flush the toilet at night, when we're upstairs, or Lily will dial nine-one-one."

"I think this is going to work! Case, you're good at this." Ned sounded surprised.

"I know!" Case sounded a little surprised himself. "Scary, isn't it?"

# 11

## WHERE'S NED?

"Mrs. Hill? It's Louise Mantera from Human Services calling on Monday afternoon. I'm Ned Ryan's social worker. We've had to turn in a missing persons report on him, but I'm hoping Ned's okay and still in the area. I'd like to talk to your son Casey to see if he can help us. I'll call again tonight."

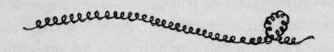

Mrs. Hill turned a serious face to her son, her finger still on the message button. "Casey?" she said quietly. "Did you know Ned was missing?"

"I know he wasn't in school last week," Case

said. He avoided her eyes and headed for the refrigerator to pour a glass of milk. Lily watched him from the big chair, silent for once. "I figured it had something to do with that foster home, I guess," he said over his shoulder.

"Did Ned say he was having trouble there? Could he have run away?" his mother persisted.

"I don't really know, Mom. I didn't get a chance to talk to him much. Don't forget, we're not taking the same bus anymore." Case gulped the milk and set the empty glass in the sink. Why didn't she quit asking all these questions? Why couldn't she just start making dinner?

"Maybe Ned hated it at the foster home," Lily said. "I don't blame him for being a missing person."

"Well, a missing persons report means the police are involved now," Mrs. Hill said, and she bit her lower lip.

"Are they going to arrest Ned?" Lily asked worriedly. "Maybe they'll put him in jail with Daddy!"

"I don't see why that social worker had to call the police," Case said, scared. "Why'd she have to go do that? What did she think, that Ned was kidnapped?"

"It's the law, Case, if a person is missing.

Especially if a child is missing. Ned *could* have been kidnapped—there could be foul play."

"What's foul play?" Lily asked.

"That's like if someone commits a crime. The police have to be concerned that someone might try to hurt Ned."

"I'm sure he's okay," Case said.

"I hope so, but I'm afraid we can't be certain of that at all," his mother said. "We'll stay home tonight, until Ms. Mantera calls back. Maybe something you say can help her find Ned, Case."

"But I thought we were walking Champion over to Mrs. Donovan's shop after dinner to see Mr. Fluff in the window," Lily objected. "And then we were getting ice cream!"

"We can see Casey's window tomorrow, baby. Ned comes first."

"I—I'll go downstairs and get Champion anyway," Case said, edging toward the door. "While you're fixing dinner."

"But what if the social worker calls?" Mrs. Hill said.

"I'll go get Champion!" Lily said, jumping up from the big squashy chair.

"No!" Case cried. "No," he said, trying to act calmer. "He's used to me, and anyway, Buddy's door sticks. I'll go—it'll just take a minute. You can yell down the stairs if that lady calls."

"Well, make it quick, Casey. Oh, poor Ned!"

Case let himself in Buddy's apartment, then locked the door behind him. Champion ran over, wagging his tail. "Hi, boy," Case said, ruffling the dog's fur. Ned came out of the bedroom, his hair mussed and his cheek imprinted with wavy lines from Buddy's bedspread. "You were asleep?" Case asked, surprised.

Ned nodded. "There's nothing else to do—"

"Listen," Case interrupted, "there's a problem, maybe. That social worker turned in a missing persons report on you to the police."

"The police! Oh, great," Ned said with a groan. "Like I didn't have enough trouble."

"I don't know yet how hard they're looking for you. She's going to call me back tonight. My mom's all freaking out."

"Oh, no," Ned said, his thin face growing pale. "What about my Granny? Do you think they told her yet?"

"Maybe. It depends on how she's doing in the hospital, I guess."

"But she'll be so worried!"

"I'll think of something, don't panic. Listen," Case said again, "I have to get back upstairs, before Lily comes down. I'll bring Champion back in a couple of hours. Did you eat dinner?"

"Sort of. I ate something before I fell asleep, I think."

"I'll get you more food tomorrow, but I'm saving as much money as I can for when Buddy gets home and you have to go someplace else."

"My running-away fund," Ned said, his smile a little weak.

"Whatever. But Mrs. Donovan gave me an extra twenty bucks for that window display, so that's good anyway."

"Case, you're giving me all your money," Ned said slowly.

"That's okay. It's just money."

"Well, thanks."

Champion ran to Buddy's front door and sniffed at the floor. "Casey," a little voice outside called, "Mom wants you. Dinner!"

"It's Lily," Case whispered. "Quick, hide in the bedroom. I'll be back later." He let himself out the door and watched as Lily threw her arms around Champion. The big dog was overjoyed to see her and licked her small face.

"Who were you talking to in there?" Lily asked, looking up at him.

"Who do you think? I was talking to Champion."

"Oh," Lily said, as if that made perfect sense. Then the three of them scrambled up the steep wooden stairs.

The Hills had just finished eating when the phone rang. Lily had already been excused from the table and was playing on the floor with her dolls.

"I'll get it," Case's mother said. Case dragged his fork through some leftover ketchup on his plate, dreading what would probably come next. Sure enough, it was for him. His mother handed him the phone.

"Casey?" a raspy voice said. "This is Louise Mantera, Ned's social worker. Did he tell you about me?"

"Sort of. He said someone picked him up at school that day his Granny got sick."

"That was me. Casey, we're very concerned about Ned. You know he disappeared from family court last Friday, right before the hearing?"

"He did?" Case said, not sure if she was asking a question or making a statement.

"Yes. I don't know why—it was just a routine hearing. Did Ned say anything to you at school?"

"About what?"

"Oh, about his grandmother, or the foster home, or anything like that. Was there something that was bothering him?"

*Only his life,* Case thought.

"Casey?"

"He said he liked his foster home okay, so far."

"That's what we thought. Mrs. Juniper is terribly worried about Ned, of course, and little Franklin is brokenhearted. He took to Ned right away."

"Oh," Case said.

"That's why I'm so concerned. If nothing was wrong, then where's Ned? We have to assume he's in some danger."

"Danger?"

"The police will probably be asking you some questions, Casey. About where Ned likes to hang out, and so on. I want you to be sure to cooperate with them."

Case's heart thudded as he pictured himself trying to answer police questions. He imagined his father saying, *Don't forget, you answer to me, kid. And*

*I don't want any son of mine squealing to the cops.* People said that on TV, anyway.

"Casey? You *will* cooperate, won't you?"

"Sure," he said, "but I don't think I can really help any."

Louise Mantera sighed. "It's rough out there, Casey. Even if Ned just ran away, he'll be in trouble, fast. I want you to call me if you hear the slightest thing, all right?"

"Okay," he said. "Uh, Ms. Mantera?" he asked, after she had given him her phone number. "Did you tell Ned's Granny yet that he was missing?"

"Yes. I went over to the hospital Friday afternoon. It was very hard, Casey. She feels like it's all her fault."

"*Her* fault? How could it be her fault?"

"For getting sick in the first place, I guess. Sometimes people blame themselves for things at the drop of a hat. *Some* people. Other people never blame themselves for anything, though, so I guess it evens out." She gave a tired laugh.

"Uh, Ms. Mantera?" Case said again. "Ned said something at school about his mother. That you were looking for her."

"How did he know that?"

"I don't know. Did you find her, though?"

"Yes, we located her, in Galveston. Texas."

"Oh," said Case. *So Ned was right,* he thought. *They did find her—and pretty fast, too.*

"Why, Casey? Do you think Ned might be trying to get to Texas, to be with his mother?"

"I don't think so," Case said. "I seriously doubt it."

"Let's hope not," the social worker said. "That's *all* Ned needs," she added under her breath.

"Well," Case said, desperate to end the conversation, "I have to hang up now. I've got a lot of homework and stuff."

"Okay, Casey," Ms. Mantera said. "You call me if you hear anything."

"All right, I will," Case agreed, glancing at his mom as she quietly cleared the table.

*But don't hold your breath, lady,* he thought, hanging up the phone.

Case sat on his bed, the striped alcove curtains pulled shut. His mind was racing. *My rook's in Cape May,* he thought, *visiting his sister. I've moved Ned into the fortress. So there's a safe corner for the king—for a week anyway. Now if I can only keep him from getting*

*trapped! Hey, I LIKE castling. Let's just hope it works. Maybe I wouldn't be so bad at chess after all!*

Case turned and twisted his covers up over his head like a hood. *Even if this doesn't save Ned, it's better than us kids just being pawns all the time. And Ned can hardly believe I'm doing it—at least someone is fighting for him! Now, if I could only figure out what the next move's going to be...*

# 12

## THE SEXIST PIG

"Um, Case? This is Ellie Lane. Could you call me tonight? It's important. Thanks. Bye!"

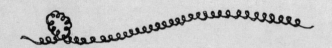

Case waited until after dinner to call, when his mother was in the bathroom with Lily. Champion was keeping them company. It was Tuesday, shampoo night, and he knew it would be a long time before they emerged. He could hear muffled squawks, yelps, and thuds as he dialed Ellie's number.

"Hello?" Ellie answered.

"Hi, it's me," Case said. They hadn't spoken to one another since their strained conversation in the cafeteria on Friday. What did she want from him, anyway? Couldn't she take a hint?

"Oh. Thanks for calling back," Ellie said.

"That's okay. You said it was important?"

"It is. Um—can you talk now? I mean, is it private there?"

"Yeah. Is it private with you?"

"It's fine. My mother is having coffee with a neighbor, and my dad's out," Ellie said.

"Oh."

"Listen—it's about Ned," Ellie said in a rush. "I got called into Mr. Nava's office today. Did you?"

Mr. Nava was the assistant principal at Ben Franklin Middle School. He was a tall, serious man—totally without any sense of humor, as far as Case could tell—who stalked the halls of Ben Franklin like a giant bird, alert for trouble. "No, I didn't get called in yet," Case said. They had wanted to talk to Ellie and not to him! "Why? What did he want?"

"This policeman was there, asking questions. He wanted to know if I knew where Ned was, or if I'd heard from him, or anything."

"So what'd you say?"

"I told him no."

"Oh. That's good," Case said. "I mean, it's the truth anyway."

"But it isn't the truth!" Ellie said.

"What?" Case couldn't believe what he was hearing.

"Ned called me yesterday afternoon," she said, her voice low.

"You're kidding." Case was astounded. Ned hadn't said a word to him about calling Ellie. Was she making it up?

"No, I'm not kidding," Ellie said, a little edge sounding in her voice.

"But what did he say?" Case asked. "Did he tell you where he is?"

"He said you know where he is, Case. He said you were helping him hide out. That he's okay, though."

Case was silent. Thoughts whirled in his head, but he couldn't speak.

"Why didn't you tell me, Case? I've been so scared!"

"I— We had to keep it a secret. He's okay, though."

"Sure, for now, maybe," Ellie said.

"What else did he tell you?"

"He told me about his mother, and how he doesn't want to go back to Texas, ever. And he's worried about his Granny, that all this will make her worse."

106

"I know," Case said. "I'm worried about that too."

"You lied to me about Ned and his Granny, Case," Ellie said. "But why?"

"I don't know," Case said. "I—I guess I figured we could just take care of it ourselves, me and Ned. We always did okay before." *Without you*, he added to himself.

There was a pause; then Ellie asked, "So what are we going to do now?"

"We?"

"I want to do something too," Ellie said. "I want to help."

"Like how?"

"I don't know. I could do whatever you're doing. Bring him food and things."

"I don't think we need any help," Case said, stubborn. "Anyway, you could get in trouble. I bet you've never been in trouble before in your life!" He almost laughed at the idea—Ellie Lane, Little Miss Perfect!

"Not much trouble," she admitted. "But this is important."

"Well, I don't know," Case said. "This stuff is kind of hard. I'm not sure—"

"You want to be the only one to help him,

is that it? Poor pathetic Ned, and you're the hero?"

"No!" Case objected. "That's just dumb. And anyway, Ned's not pathetic." How could she say that? Ned just needed his help, that was all. *His* help.

"It makes you feel good, doesn't it, hiding him?" Ellie said. "Like he has to count on you for everything. But I'm his friend too. Or is that it, that I'm a girl? You just assume I'm going to goof everything up if I try to help!"

"It's not like that," Case said, angry. "I'd let you help, but you probably couldn't do it. You'd have to sneak around, and maybe lie."

"And you won't even give me a chance, will you?" Ellie said flatly. "You want to help Ned all by yourself, don't you? Well, you don't own him, Case."

"It's not like that," Case repeated. He couldn't think of anything else to say.

"So let me help."

Case sighed. "Well..." He thought hard for a moment, trying to think of something he could let her do. Anything to make her stop talking! Ellie was so smart, Case thought, but she didn't have a clue about some things. Like why he might not want her hanging out with Ned, for instance.

Then he made up his mind: "I know something you could do," he said, "if you really want to help. How good are you at changing your voice?"

"You mean like doing imitations?"

"Well, imitating a grownup anyway."

"I believe I could manage that, young man!" Ellie said, suddenly sounding much older. Case laughed a little, in spite of being mad at her. "Why?" she added in her regular voice.

"Because I have an idea. It'll be your first assignment. I'll call you back in half an hour, after I pry some information from my mom. I'll give you a phone number to call then and tell you what message to leave when you call it."

"Okay," she said, a little breathless. "My mother will probably be home when you call, though," she warned.

"Just tell her it's for homework," Case said, laughing a little. "Your first lie."

Ellie laughed too. "Okay. And Case—"

"What?"

"Thanks for letting me help. I won't let you guys down."

Case hung up, feeling shaken. All that stuff Ellie had said about Case getting to feel good because

he was the one hiding Ned. Where did she get that? Ellie didn't have the slightest idea what he was feeling!

And then her saying he wouldn't let her help just because she was a girl. He hated stuff like that! He'd let her help, hadn't he? *Let's just see how she likes it,* he thought. *She'll see it's not all fun and games.*

And how could she have said he wanted Ned to have to count on him? That wasn't fair! It wasn't his fault Ned didn't have that many friends.

Well, that had been true last fall anyway. But was Ned still so unpopular? Case flopped down on his bed, pulled the curtains shut, and thought...

After all, here was Ellie Lane, *his* Ellie Lane, calling because she was worried about Ned. She and Ned were actually friends—it was true! Case remembered when he had been Ned's only friend, just about. Why hadn't Ned ever mentioned Ellie before? What else didn't he—Case—know about Ned? Or about Ellie?

An hour later, he was still awake. *Girls,* he thought, disgusted. He remembered earlier that evening, on the way home before dinner. They had gone to see his new display window at

Treasure. Trove. He had thought everyone would love it, especially Lily.

But no. "I want him back!" Lily had roared after taking one look at the window.

"Lily, calm down. Mr. Fluff is the star of Casey's window—he looks great, baby," Mrs. Hill said.

"He doesn't look great, he looks stupid. He's wearing an apron. I want him back!"

"It's for spring cleaning, Lily," Case explained. "Get it?" Case had—with help—moved a huge old clock from the storeroom into the shop window. It was from a tower that had been torn down, and it stood taller than Case on its curved iron frame. In front of it, Case had placed a red plastic bucket on a wooden ladder. He had suspended Mr. Fluff, Lily's prized stuffed animal, from the top of the clock. It looked as if he was dusting the face of the clock with a red and white polka-dot rag. "Yeah, he's wearing an apron," Case admitted, "but it's like the sign says: *It's Time for Spring Cleaning!* Don't you get it?"

"I get it, I get it! But Mr. Fluff is a *boy*," Lily yelled, hands on her hips.

"He's a stuffed animal!" Case shouted back.

"Wait a minute, hold on," their mother said.

"Lily, so what if he's a boy? Don't boys clean, too?"

"No," she said firmly, indignant. "Not wearing aprons anyway."

"Lily Hill, I can't believe my ears," Mrs. Hill said. "Where did you get such an idea?"

"It's not an idea, it's the truth. Girls clean."

"And what do boys do?"

"They work."

"Lily, cleaning is work. And if you're talking about a paying job, I work," her mother said, frustrated.

"You do now. Not before Daddy went to jail, though. And I liked it better then."

"That's beside the point, Lily. Lots of women work now. Most women, in fact—and lots of men clean."

"Not Daddy. He never wore an apron in his whole life. Case is just trying to make Mr. Fluff look dumb in front of everyone."

"I thought you'd like it," Case said. "Mrs. Donovan loves it. And I gave you credit—did you see the sign I made thanking you?"

Lily nodded. "You're welcome. But I still want him back."

"Mom," Case said, "Mrs. Donovan wants to

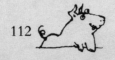

112

keep the display up a few weeks at least! I can't take it apart now."

"Lily," Mrs. Hill reasoned, "you said Case could use your kitty for the window."

"Not wearing an apron, I didn't."

"What if he took the apron off? Mr. Fluff could be like—like a clock cleaner!"

Lily thought about this. "Is that a boy job?" she finally asked.

"My sister the sexist pig," Case said, rolling his eyes. "I thought you said you wanted to be in business."

"Case, you're not helping here," his mother said.

"Sorry."

"What about it, Lily?" Mrs. Hill asked. "Can Mr. Fluff stay in the window?"

"Well, I guess so," Lily said, reluctant to give up the fight. "As long as everyone knows he's really a boy."

"Anyone named 'Mister' is a boy," her mother assured her.

"I don't know about the 'Fluff' part, though," Case said.

"That's his *name*, Casey," Lily had said in her most sarcastic voice. "Duh!"

* * *

*So it's not just boys saying girls can't do things,* Case thought now as he flutter-kicked his legs, trying to untangle the covers. *I mean, look at Lily! She was saying boys can't do girl things. And besides— that's not why I didn't want Ellie to help. I just wanted to keep things simple, that's all. Anyway, this is my game...*

"Did you hear about Ned Ryan?" Bryan DeLillo asked Case in the hall at school the next day. It was the break between second and third periods. Two boys stood right behind Bryan, listening avidly to every word. Around them, kids churned up and down the halls, hurrying to class.

Case slammed the battered door to his locker shut, hoping everything jammed inside wouldn't fall out on him next time he opened it. He twirled the lock. "No, what about him?" he asked.

"You're his friend, I thought you'd know," Bryan said, stalling. When he had a morsel of news, he liked to get all the attention he could.

"Know about what?" Case repeated, impatient. "Come on, the bell's about to ring."

"About that foster home," one of the other kids said.

"What about it?"

"You know, how they were all mean to him and everything," Bryan said, excited. "I heard they wouldn't even let him keep his dog, or any of his own clothes! No wonder he ran away."

"Well, a neighbor has the dog for now," Case began.

But Bryan wasn't even listening. "And Ned must have really caused trouble," he was saying, "because I heard they were making him go to *court*."

"Oooh—busted!" one of the kids said as he laughed and shook his head.

"I always thought Ned was kind of a wuss, though," the other kid said, looking skeptical.

Bryan lowered his voice and squinted his eyes. "I guess they just pushed him too far," he said. "Poor guy. Who knows where he is by now."

# 13

## THE NEXT MOVE

"Hello? Hello? This is Hazel Ryan calling on Tuesday, I think. Or is this Wednesday? The nurse told me a woman called saying Neddy is all right. Was that you? Is my Neddy with you? I'm praying it's true. Please call when you can. Goodbye!"

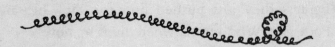

Mrs. Hill frowned and replayed the message. "What on earth?" Case busied himself checking the mail. "Casey," his mother said, "did you hear anything at school about Ned turning up?"

"Uh, no," Case replied. "I didn't hear anything."

"Maybe it was the police who called her," Lily

said, matching her mother's frown. She put her hands on her hips. "I bet they arrested Ned."

"Or maybe it was the social worker who called," Mrs. Hill said. "What was her name again?"

"I forget," Case said firmly.

"Well, I have it here somewhere," she muttered as she rummaged through a pile of papers near the phone. "And her home phone number, too."

"I'm going to go walk Champion," Case announced, edging toward the door.

"And then bring him up here, okay?" Lily said. "Tell him we're having burritos!"

"We're having burritos *after* I call the social worker and Mrs. Ryan," her mother corrected her. "If Ned's okay, I want to know about it." Case slipped out of the apartment and ran downstairs.

Ned was hanging up Buddy's phone as Case let himself in. Champion bounded over to greet him. "Hi," Ned said, with a guilty look at the phone.

"Hi. Who were you talking to?"

"A friend. Ellie, from school."

Casey scowled, jealous. "I don't think it's such a great idea for you to be using the phone. What if Buddy calls and gets a busy signal?"

"Why would he call his own house?"

"I don't know. He might."

117

"That would be kind of goofy, Case," Ned said.

"I still don't think it's such a great idea to use the phone. How come you need to talk to Ellie, anyway? I can bring her a message at school, if you write it down."

"It's really lonely down here, Case. I mean, I'm grateful and everything, but it's Wednesday. I've been shut up four and a half days already. No sunshine, no lights, no nothing. I feel like I'm turning into a bat."

"It's better than being out on the street, isn't it?" Case asked.

"I'm not complaining," Ned said. He flopped down on one of Buddy's leather chairs. It creaked a little.

"Well, what'd she have to say? Ellie?" Case asked, drawing his finger through the dust on a glass tabletop.

"She said how she's helping you and everything. You never told me, Case."

"She only did that one thing so far," Case said. "One little thing, and I was going to mention it." He went into the kitchen and emptied Champion's water bowl into the sink, which was filled with dirty dishes, then refilled it.

"But I don't want her getting into any trouble because of me," Ned said, his voice loud over the running water.

"She wanted to help," Case said. "And keep it down, will you? Don't talk so loud."

"Well, but did Granny really get Ellie's message that I'm okay?" Ned asked, his voice a little lower.

"Sort of. A nurse got it, anyway. Your Granny thought it was probably my mom who called. Mom's upstairs trying to track down who really did it." Case walked back into the living room and straightened a pile of magazines on the coffee table. It was hard to remember exactly how Buddy had left them.

"Do you think Granny believed it, though?" Ned asked solemnly.

"She sounded relieved on the answering machine," Case said.

"For now anyway."

"Hey, I finally got called into Nava's office today," Case said, trying to change the subject. "This guy from the police was there. He was asking me all these questions."

"Yeah, Ellie said they called her in, too." Ned laughed a little. "All year, no one knew I was even

119

in that school, practically, but now that I'm a missing person, they're finally noticing me."

Case nodded. "All the kids are talking. The ones in sixth grade anyway."

"Like what do they say?"

"Well, some of them think you're dead," Case admitted, picking at a loose flap of rubber on one of his sneakers.

"Dead!" Ned was alarmed. "How come they think that?"

"Oh, you know, all those stray maniacs on the loose," Case said with a shrug. "It's something for them to talk about anyway. Bryan the Mouth is in hog heaven."

"Yeah, he would be. What is he saying?"

"That you ran away somewhere because of the cruel foster home. He says he doesn't blame you."

"But that's not true," Ned said. "Mrs. Juniper was nice."

"Well, I'm just saying," Case said.

"So what did the police ask you?"

"Oh, when I saw you last, where you like to hang out, stuff like that. I told them I pretty much lost track of you after your Granny got sick."

"Do you think they believed you?"

"Yeah," Case said, a little proud. "I looked them right in the eye."

"So now what?" Ned asked, getting up and starting to pace. "What's the next move?"

"Buddy comes back on Saturday, so I'll have to get you out of here by Friday night," Case said as if thinking aloud.

"Maybe I should just turn myself in to that social worker," Ned said slowly, "and go back to Mrs. Juniper's. Take my chances."

"No! I mean, I don't think so," Case said. He didn't want Ned to do that—not when he had everything all planned. "They might not let you go back to Mrs. Juniper's house," he explained. "I didn't tell you, but they found your mom."

"They did? Oh, no," Ned said. "When?"

"A couple of days ago. She's in Galveston."

Ned nodded, glum. "That's pretty near Houston. I knew they'd find her," he added, bitter. "So that means I can't ever go back to Mrs. Juniper's now. Goodbye, Mrs. Juniper, goodbye, Franklin."

Case was silent. A week ago Ned hadn't even known those people, he thought.

"But where will I go?" Ned was asking.

"I think—I'm pretty sure they're watching your Granny's house," Case said. "I walked by and saw someone coming out the door. So that's out."

"Oh, I wish I was bigger," Ned said. "I could go somewhere and get a job. Lie about my age."

"Well, you're *not* bigger," Case said. "You're even shorter than me. Hey, that's one of the reasons I like you," he kidded, trying to cheer Ned up.

"Case, this is serious," Ned said, flinging himself onto Buddy's sofa. "What am I going to do? Where will I go?"

"We have two possibilities, the way I see it," Case said, getting serious. "There's school, or there's Mrs. Donovan's shop."

"The shop?" Ned asked. "But what would she say?"

"She wouldn't even know. You'd hide back in the storeroom," Case explained. "She doesn't like to go back there much because of the spiders."

"Spiders! Case, that doesn't sound so wonderful to me, either."

"They're not *harmful* spiders," Case assured him, "just big."

"So I don't get poisoned, I have a heart attack. Great, Case. Anyway, what would I eat? Where would I go to the bathroom?"

"I'd bring sandwiches after school, and you'd have to wait until night to use the toilet."

"Case!"

"I know, I know, it's not perfect," Case said hastily.

"I don't expect it to be perfect, but..."

"That leaves school," Case said. He looked at Ned, waiting for his reaction. This was his most daring plan yet!

Ned gaped at him. "I thought you were joking about that. You mean, just go back?"

Case nodded. "Not to classes. You'd have to hide out during classes."

"Where?"

"I'll find some places, don't worry."

"But isn't it kind of risky, hiding out at school?"

"Sure, but in a way it's perfect. It would serve them right at Ben Franklin. Like you said, no one even knew you were there before. It's not like they cared about you or your problems. Nava probably can't even remember what you look like!"

"But the kids will know it's me."

"Some of them might," Case said, "but I'll take care of that."

"How?" Ned asked.

"Disguises! Maybe I'll let Ellie help," he added

grudgingly. "She did okay with that phone call."

"You know something? It's good," Ned said, beginning to smile. "It's like *The Phantom of the Opera*, kind of."

Case frowned as he tried to remember the story.

"You know," Ned said, "where that guy with the mask hides out right there in the opera house? It's brilliant, Case. How long do you think we could pull it off?"

"A while. Long enough for me to figure out the move after that anyway."

"Case, you've got guts."

"Well, whatever," Case said modestly. "You're the one who's going to have to do it, don't forget. Hey, I've got to take this dog out before he explodes. And Ned—"

"Yeah?"

"Stay off the phone, okay? It could ruin the plan."

"Okay, Case. Sorry."

# 14

## APPLESAUCE

"Hello, Hills! It's Louise Mantera calling again. Ned's social worker, remember? It's—ah—Thursday afternoon. I need to talk to Case again. Could I come by tonight, maybe? I'll call you at work, Mrs. Hill, and arrange a time. I've got that number back at the office. See you soon, then."

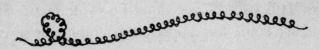

"She's coming here?" Case asked, horrified. "But why? I told her everything—and the police, too."

"Casey, calm down. I'm sure Ms. Mantera just has some follow-up questions. Now hang up your jacket—it's dripping all over the floor. I'm turning up the heat in here."

"This is like on TV, where they come back and

arrest the guy," Lily said, eyes shining. "But what did you do?"

"Nothing!" Case said. "Mom, why didn't you tell me she was coming?"

"I didn't know about it until late this afternoon, Case, and I forgot to tell you when we were on our way home."

"She forgot a strange lady was coming over to interrogate her only son," Case said to Lily.

Mrs. Hill ignored this comment and continued to speak. "I invited her to share supper with us, but—"

"You invited her to eat? Mom!" Case moaned. "It's not like this is a party or something."

"But it's not like you've done anything wrong," Mrs. Hill said. "Case, don't be so dramatic. She couldn't come for supper. She's coming at seven-thirty."

"Just in time for my bath," Lily said happily. She sat down in front of the radiator as if it were a fireplace and held her hands up to the warmth.

"But I have homework, Mom. Lots of home-work. Maybe you better call her back and cancel."

"And maybe you can help your sister set the table, Mr. Hill, once she gets warmed up. This subject is closed."

"I'll talk to her when she comes," Lily said. "Don't worry. I like company."

"No, no, no, no, NO!" the little girl yelled. "Not shampoo night again!" She clung like a magnet to the big chair near the telephone. "We just had a shampoo night." Mrs. Hill stood near the bathroom door, hands on her hips. Worried, Champion tried to creep under the Hills' kitchen table, where Louise Mantera and Case were seated.

"Well," Mrs. Hill said, "if you hadn't gotten Play-Doh in your hair, we wouldn't have to wash it again so soon. Honestly, Lily. I didn't even see it at first, but it's getting harder by the minute. You're getting a little old for this."

"It was Daisy Greenough, she did it! She said, 'Want a cupcake?' Then she smooshed it into my hair. Only it was Play-Doh."

"Why would she do such a thing?"

"Because she hates my guts, that's why."

"Lily, where on earth did you ever hear such an expression?" Mrs. Hill exclaimed.

"Everybody says it, and it's true! You don't know her. She—"

Case looked down at his hands: they were folded neatly on the shiny Formica tabletop.

Ms. Mantera tapped a pencil against her notebook and bit her lower lip as she watched Lily.

"I'm sorry," Mrs. Hill called over to her. "I'll try to keep the noise down once we're in the bathroom, so you two can talk."

"Good luck," Case said. "We'll be lucky if we can hear anything. It's only going to get worse. Maybe we should do this another time."

Ms. Mantera glanced around the small apartment as if looking for a quieter place she and Casey could talk. Her brown eyes seemed to take in every detail. "I know," Mrs. Hill said suddenly. "Buddy's apartment! Case, you take Ms. Mantera downstairs. It'll be nice and quiet there, and I know Buddy wouldn't mind. He's our landlord, but he's out of town," she added to Ms. Mantera.

"No! We can't do that," Case said, panicked.

"Why not? It's the perfect solution. Come on back up when the howling stops, both of you. We'll all have some applesauce."

Case walked slowly, heavily down the steep flight of stairs. "It's right down here," he called out over his shoulder. At Buddy's front door, Case fumbled with the lock.

"Want me to try?" Ms. Mantera asked. She reached a slim brown hand toward the key.

"No, that's okay," Case said, shaking the door a little. "It always does this." He pushed his way in and held his breath as he looked around the dark apartment. "Here we are," he said loudly. There was no sign of Ned, thank goodness. The bedroom door was open a little, though, and so was the bathroom door.

Ms. Mantera turned on some lights, walked over to Buddy's sofa, and sat down. "Now, Casey," she said, opening her notebook.

"Yes, ma'am?" Casey said. He wiped his hands on his sweatshirt and sat at the far end of the sofa.

"Let's see," she said, flipping through some pages. "Oh, here we are. Someone telephoned Ned's grandmother at the hospital, or they tried to anyway."

"They did?"

"Yes, saying Ned is safe. Nothing more than that." She looked up quickly and watched Case's expression.

He kept his face still. "They didn't say where Ned was?"

"No, just that he's all right."

129

"Well, that's good, isn't it? Maybe you can stop looking for him now."

"It doesn't work like that, Casey," Ms. Mantera said, shaking her head. Her black hair was so short—shorter than his, even—that it didn't move, but her dangling earrings caught the light. "I mean, I feel a little better about things, a *little* better, but Ned's still gone, isn't he?"

"Oh. Yeah." Case stretched a leg out and examined his sneaker. "So I guess Ned's mom is all worried now?"

"His mother?"

"In Texas."

"I know she's in Texas, Casey. But she isn't especially worried. She has other things on her mind."

"Oh, yeah," Case repeated.

"So you know about Ned's mom, her situation? Did Ned talk about it?"

"No," Case said hastily. "I just meant I know moms worry a lot. In general." He ran his finger over the sofa's upholstery as if trying to memorize its pattern.

Ms. Mantera smiled. "I guess they do, but that's especially true for Ned's mother. Worrying in general, I mean."

"How come?" Case thought he saw Buddy's bedroom door move slightly, but he was afraid to look directly at it. He tried to ignore it.

"Well, after we located her through her driver's license, we asked a social worker there to go check things out."

"To see if she wanted Ned?"

"And to see if Ned would be happy there."

"Why didn't you just ask him if he'd be happy there?"

"We didn't get the chance, Casey. Remember? He ran away."

"Would you have listened to him if he said no?"

"We would have taken it into account," Ms. Mantera said slowly, "but a lot would have depended on the Texas situation."

"You mean on whether his mother wanted him there or not. So it wouldn't have been Ned's decision, not totally."

"No," she admitted. "But that's really beside the point now. Ned is *not* going back to Texas."

"If his mom doesn't want him, that's just because she's dumb," Case said, angry. Why did poor Ned have to hear all this?

"We never asked his mother if she wanted Ned, Casey. She's got two little kids as it is, and a

boyfriend who's a drunk. The social worker really walked in on a bad scene. Ned's not going anywhere near there! I just hope he won't be too disappointed when he finds out."

"But—but what about those two little Texas kids?" Case asked. "It's not safe for them there either, is it?"

"Texas is looking into that now. All thanks to Ned, in a way."

"Yeah, I guess," Case said. "Um, so where will Ned go? If he turns up, I mean."

"Back to Mrs. Juniper's, unless he has some objection. She and Franklin would be thrilled, and his Granny would be so relieved."

"Ned wouldn't be punished for running away?"

"No. If running away becomes a chronic problem, though, he'll switch over from 'dependent' to 'delinquent,' and that's a whole different ball game. Different court system, the works."

"I don't think Ned's the type to keep on running away," Case said.

"Neither do I, from what little I saw of him. He seemed like a really nice guy."

Case definitely saw the bedroom door move a little more, and he knew his friend had overheard

132

every word they'd said. *What if Ned came out now and gave himself up? I'd probably get the blame for everything,* Case thought. *And Buddy might get in trouble too! After all, it's his apartment.*

He jumped up. "Listen," he said, "let's go back upstairs. It sounds pretty quiet up there now. I— I'll ask around, and stuff. About Ned. He's got to be somewhere."

"You get the word out, Casey. Tomorrow. I want to wrap this one up. It has the chance of a reasonably happy ending at least. Not like some of my cases." She stood up. "I'll get the lights," she said.

"That's okay. I have to bring Champion back down in about an hour—I'll turn them off then."

Later that night, Case fumbled once more with the key to Buddy's apartment. Champion had been anxious to go back downstairs, and Case didn't blame him. Ms. Mantera had stayed upstairs for a long time, yakking away with Case's mother, and then Lily had to show their guest every single doll outfit she had, including underwear. Case shuddered at the memory.

Now, Champion snuffled at the bottom of Buddy's front door, wagging his tail. "Boy, I'm glad

133

I didn't have to count on *you* to keep a secret," Case said. He pushed open the door.

Buddy was only a few feet away, sitting in his wheelchair. Waiting.

Case hung back in the doorway as Champion rushed forward in greeting. "Hey, Champ," Buddy said, "take it easy. It's really me. I'm home."

"But—it's only Thursday. You're early!" Case said.

"I thought I'd surprise everyone," Buddy said. "I guess I did," he added, raising an eyebrow. He wasn't laughing.

Case glanced toward the bedroom door, his heart thudding; then he forced his eyes back to Buddy. Maybe he didn't even know Ned was here! "So, was it a good trip?" he asked, as casually as he could.

"Quit it, Case. I know what's been going on," Buddy said, as if reading Case's mind. His dark eyes glittered; although Case had never seen him look that way before, he could tell Buddy was really angry.

"But—but where is Ned, then?" Case asked. "You didn't turn him in, did you?"

Buddy ignored Case's last question. "Ned's

sound asleep," he said. "He's exhausted. I told him I'd sleep out here tonight—the sofa folds out. You can help me set it up."

"Oh, okay." Case hurried toward the sofa, eager to do something—anything—rather than face Buddy and talk.

But Buddy had other ideas. "That can wait a minute, Case," he said. "Sit down." Case sat. "Now, what's going on? And I want it straight."

"Didn't Ned tell you?" Case asked, trying to stall a little.

"I want to hear it from you. You're the one who's supposed to be my friend, right? I trusted you—and it appears you masterminded this whole thing behind my back."

"But I had to," Case said. "Ned needed help, fast. He needed somewhere to stay."

"And you just happened to know a place," Buddy said, his face stony.

"I would have asked you, but you were gone already. And we thought they were going to send Ned back to Texas to live with his mom and her psycho boyfriend."

He didn't add that they hadn't actually known about the boyfriend—not then.

"But now they aren't going to send him there,"

Buddy stated. Ned had obviously told him everything.

"Well, no. But we only found that out tonight. Didn't Ned tell you about the social worker lady coming here?"

Buddy nodded. "So everything worked out pretty well, for Ned and for you, too, Case. Ned's really grateful—he thinks you're a hero. You guys were lucky."

"And the social worker doesn't know Ned was staying here," Case said, "so you won't get in any trouble either."

Buddy smiled a little and raised a shaggy eyebrow. "From what you guys have told me, it's hard to say what the social worker knows. But so far, at least, we're all in the clear."

"I didn't ever mean to get you involved," Case said sheepishly.

"Well, I am involved," Buddy said. "You made sure of that, regardless of what you meant to do. But if you can get Ned back safely to his foster home, you might just pull this off without getting all of us in any deeper."

"There are other places besides the foster home that he could go," Case said. "I mean, we were

going to have to leave here pretty soon anyway. Tomorrow, in fact."

"Where else were you planning on hiding him?"

"Oh, there's a couple of places," Case said, boasting a little.

"Ned hates foster care that much?" Buddy asked.

"Well, not really," Case admitted. "He sort of likes it."

"So who were you going to do this for, Case? Yourself?"

"No!" Case said. "I just— The social worker didn't know he was going to like his foster home. It could have been terrible!"

"But it's not," Buddy stated.

"Well, no."

"So there's no reason for him not to go back. Now what's your plan, Case? How are you going to get him back there?"

"Uh, maybe he could call a taxi, after we all leave tomorrow morning?" Case said, making it sound like a question. "All us Hills, I mean."

"Ned has the address of the foster home?"

"Yeah. It's not too far from Ben Franklin. How much would a ride like that cost, do you think?"

"Under ten dollars, plus tip," Buddy said. "The driver will probably ask to see the money first, since Ned's a kid. And Ned shouldn't give him too big a tip or the driver will wonder about him, remember him."

"How much of a tip, then?"

"Fifteen percent of the fare. Can Ned figure that out?"

Case laughed, then nodded. "Ned could probably figure out the square root of the fare."

"Good," Buddy said, chuckling.

Case was relieved to hear him laugh again. "But won't the driver remember where he picked Ned up?" he asked. "If anyone investigates, I mean. They could trace him back here."

"The taxi doesn't have to come directly here. There's always a line of cabs waiting over near Headhouse Square."

"Oh, yeah. I've seen them."

"Champion and I will just happen to walk over there too, tomorrow morning, to make sure there's no hitch. I think midmorning would be best."

"I do too," Case agreed. He glanced toward the ceiling and said, "We better set up the sofa bed now. I have to get back upstairs before Mom comes looking for me."

"Pile the cushions over there in the corner," Buddy said. "Then move the coffee table. You yank that tab in the middle to pull out the bed. And there's a pillow and quilt in the linen closet—that's all I'll need. Now, go," he said, when Case had finished.

"Okay. Buddy—listen, I never meant to trick you," Case said. "That wasn't part of my plan. It just happened. I'm really sorry."

"But you weren't sure I'd be on your side, either, were you? Not one hundred percent sure."

"I guess not," Case admitted.

"That's okay, Case. I think you guys were in a position where you felt you couldn't really trust anyone."

"Well, we couldn't," Case said. "Everyone was seeing Ned's situation the same way. No one was asking him what *he* wanted."

Buddy shrugged and smiled sadly. "'Everyone' being us so-called grownups, I suppose. Well, maybe you were right," he said. "Maybe it was just as well I didn't know. I might have felt compelled to turn Ned in."

"But you didn't, not tonight," Case objected.

"No, I didn't tonight. So I guess you can trust me a little at least."

"I trust you a lot," Case said.

"Well, it looks like you may pull this whole thing off, Case."

"Tell me that tomorrow, and maybe I'll believe you."

# 15

## NEW FRIENDS

"Hi, it's me, Ned. I'm calling on Friday afternoon. I'm back at Mrs. Juniper's. Quit it, Franklin! Um, I'm sorry if you were worried about me, but everything's okay now. Mrs. Juniper wants to invite you all over for dinner tomorrow night. She'll call later, but I hope you can come. I have to hang up, we're going to visit my Granny now and then go pick up Lacy. Mrs. Juniper says she can stay here!"

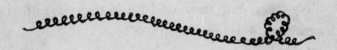

"Ned's alive!" Lily said, and she burst into tears.

"Baby," her mother said. "Oh, poor Lily. I was worried about him, too."

"I want to see him again," Lily said with a hiccup.

"We will, tomorrow," Case said, "if we go over there for dinner. Can we, Mom?"

"I don't see why not," his mother said slowly. "Anything we can do to help Ned settle in there. I want him to stay put this time."

"I don't think that's going to be a problem," Case said. "He told me before he ran away that he likes it okay. There's even a baby there, and a little kid named Franklin, who's six."

"That's not so little, Case," Lily said. "I'm six."

"Sorry. I keep forgetting," Case said.

"Is Franklin a boy or a girl?" Lily asked, frowning.

"A boy. Why?"

"Because I don't want Ned to have a little sister."

"Lily," Case said, "Franklin and Ned aren't related. They aren't brothers."

"Not yet, but they will be if they live in the same house. Tell him, Mommy."

"I think you just did."

"Lily, why don't you want Ned to have a little sister?" Case asked, curious.

Lily blushed. "*I* want to be Ned's sister. He's your best friend, Case. You guys can share. Okay?"

"Okay. I'll tell Ned if he ever needs a little sister, there's enough of you to go around."

"And then some!" their mother said, hugging them both.

"So are you going?" Ellie Lane asked later that night over the phone. Case had called her to say that everything had turned out okay.

"What?" Case asked, trying to hear over Lily's television show.

"Are you going to dinner at Ned's new house tomorrow?"

"Yeah. It'll be weird seeing Ned in a different place, with different people all around."

"Well, say hi for me," Ellie said, gloomy.

Case clamped his hand over one ear, trying to hear her better. "What's the matter?" he finally asked. He was almost afraid to hear what she would say. Just how much did she like Ned, anyway?

"I hoped Ned would be back in school by now, that's all," Ellie said.

"He'll be back the Monday after spring vacation," Case reassured her. "That's only one more week. His Granny is moving into a nursing home tomorrow, and Ned's going to help that Corporation for Seniors lady get some of her stuff from their old house in the morning."

"That's good, I guess," Ellie said. "Well, I'll see him during vacation anyway."

"You will?" Case asked, hoping his voice wasn't giving him away.

"Yeah. We're going to go play chess in JFK Park. If it ever stops raining, that is."

"Oh," Case said.

"You can come too, if you want," Ellie suggested. "I don't mind. We can take turns playing each other."

"I don't know," Case said, trying to imagine sharing Ellie with his best friend—and sharing Ned with Ellie. "I'm not that good a player," he added.

"Well, you aren't going to get any better sitting at home, Case. And from what I've seen lately, you might be pretty good someday."

"Really? You think so?"

"I wouldn't say it if I didn't mean it," Ellie said.

"New friends," Mrs. Juniper said the next night, clasping her dimpled hands together. "Welcome! You must be Casey." Case shook her hand and mumbled hello. Lacy barked a frenzied greeting.

"Case, you can do better than that," his mother said, laughing.

"How do you do," Case said, clearer this time.

"And oh," Mrs. Juniper continued, "this must be Lily. The precious angel!"

"How do you do," Lily said. She thought a moment, then added a curtsy.

"Such lovely manners! Oh, you'll be such a wonderful influence on Franklin. He's a little q-u-i-e-t," she whispered, spelling the word.

"He's a little quilt?" Lily asked, puzzled.

"No, he's *quiet*," Case said. "I didn't know you could spell, Lily."

"Of course I can spell. A little, anyways. I'm much better than Daisy Greenough, though. She—"

A small boy entered the room and glared at Lily, stopping her in midsentence. "And here he is," Mrs. Juniper announced. "Here's Franklin!"

"Hey, kid," Ned whispered, giving him a little shove. Franklin's face broke into a smile, and he shoved Ned back. "Meet Lily," Ned said. "Lily, this is Franklin."

"How do you do," Lily said again, prim. She skipped the curtsy, though.

"Franklin," Mrs. Juniper suggested, "maybe you'd like to show Lily your new puzzle. You could

145

work on it together. We'll go check on the baby." She and Mrs. Hill left the room, chatting like old friends.

"I'm very good at puzzles," Franklin said in a low, growly voice.

"Well, I'm very good at puzzles, too," Lily said. "And I'm the guest, so I get to go first."

"I never heard of that rule. And anyway, you don't take turns with puzzles. You just do them. *Quietly*," he added. Their voices faded as they walked down the hall.

"*King Kong Meets Godzilla,* starring Lily and Franklin," Ned said, as if reading from a movie ad. "Franklin's not as quiet as Mrs. Juniper thinks. You should hear him sometimes."

"The whole house will probably explode in about five minutes," Case said, laughing.

"I hope we get a chance to eat first. I'm starving!" Ned said. "Wait until you taste Mrs. Juniper's cooking. It's going to be a great night."

"It already is," Case said. He meant it, too.

# 16

## NEVER TROUBLE TROUBLE

"Hey, it's Buddy, calling on Sunday morning. I guess you're out now, and I know you'll be getting ready for your big Easter picnic later, but I'd like it if Case could come down for a few minutes after lunch. Oh, and Lily, you can take your time with that job I gave you. No hurry! See you later, Case. Champion sends his best."

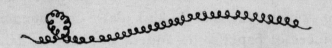

"His best what?" Lily asked.

"Casey, you can go downstairs after we eat something," Mrs. Hill said, distracted. She looked at the list she was holding and muttered, "Let's see, ham, potato salad..."

Lily looked up again from the big chair by the

telephone. "Don't forget, you have to wear your red dress, Mommy. Daddy said." She was surrounded by a fluffy pile of paper scraps.

"I'm not sure it's clean, baby."

"But he said!"

"We'll see, Lily. You have to set the table now, though. We need to eat early so I can get the picnic organized for this afternoon."

"I can't set the table now," Lily said, as if explaining something obvious. "I'm working. On my paper-shredding job—it's business."

"I thought you said the only work girls did was cleaning, Lily," Case teased her, grinning.

"Case, don't start," Mrs. Hill said.

"That was before," Lily informed her brother. "Girls need money too, Case. Duh. And anyway, this is important. I have to tear up these old pages so nobody can steal Buddy's ideas. One hundred pieces of paper," she added, impressed. "He's paying me in pennies! Case can set the table."

"*You* can set the table," Mrs. Hill corrected her. "That's your house job, Lily."

"But I don't get paid for it," Lily said, stubborn. Her face brightened. "Hey, maybe if you paid me to set the table..."

"Lily," her mother warned.

"I was only kidding," Lily said hastily. She jumped up, scattering the pile of scraps.

"I should hope so. I have enough on my mind without you going berserk," her mother said. "Everyone in a family works together for the family."

"Except Daddy," Lily said, matter-of-fact, as she counted out forks. "Are we eating fork food for lunch?"

"Yes," Mrs. Hill said. "And your father—well, he doesn't work, exactly. Not now. But he still cares about us."

*Yeah, right,* Case thought as he put away the last of the groceries. *And we'll hear all about it this afternoon. Happy Easter, everyone.*


"So Case," Buddy said after lunch, "how's every little thing?"

"The little things are great. Ned's home with Mrs. Juniper, and no one got busted. But it's the big things I worry about."

"You mean like going to see your dad at the penitentiary?"

"How'd you guess?" Case said.

"Maybe it won't be that bad," Buddy said. "I know that Christmas wasn't so hot, but—"

"Christmas was horrible," Case interrupted. "I told you. He yelled at my mom in front of everyone, and Lily cried and got sick, and then Dad blamed the whole thing on me. He said I was supposed to be the man of the house now, and obviously I wasn't up to the job."

Buddy was silent. His powerful hands rested quietly on the arms of his wheelchair, but he looked angry—angrier, even, than he had the night he'd discovered Ned in his apartment. "You do fine," he said at last.

"Oh, face it, Buddy. Nothing I do is going to be good enough for my dad. He thinks I'm like this total wimp."

"You know you're not, though. You know he's not right, Case."

"Yeah, I guess," Case said. He thought a moment, then added, "But I'm tired of kids getting pushed around all the time. You know what I mean?"

"Not exactly," Buddy said.

"Well," Case said, struggling for the words, "I thought it was just Ned, but it's not. It's everyone—it's me, too."

"Who's pushing you around?"

"Oh, well, my mom is always telling me what

to do, like I was a baby or something. But my dad's the worst. He acts like I'm this invention of his, only I didn't turn out so great."

"He does?"

"Yeah," Case said. "Like, the way he sees it, I'm this kid who lives with his mom and his little sister. I'm a kid who draws, and helps this lady in her antique shop, and doesn't do any sports, and barely has any friends..."

"And he wants you to change?"

"He sure acts like it," Case said.

"Well, I don't have any kids, but I guess some parents just get to feeling they own their kids, or something."

Suddenly Case could hear someone else saying those words. It was Ellie, he remembered, saying that Case didn't own Ned. That was weird...

"I happen to know your life is a little more exciting than the way you're telling it, Case," Buddy was saying with a grin.

"Maybe," Case admitted, "but my dad sure wouldn't think so. Any son of his should be living a different kind of life," he said, as if quoting his father's words.

"Maybe some parents just feel that way about their kids, like they invented them," Buddy repeated.

 151

"Did your dad feel like that about you?"

"Sure," Buddy said. "Even before I had the accident, he didn't understand why I'd be reading a book or writing a story when I could be outside getting fresh air and sunshine. 'Fresh air and sunshine!' Man, I hated those words."

"So what did you do?"

"I got a little fresh air and sunshine, but mostly I quietly did what I wanted. I'm glad, too, or else I'd just be a tan guy in a wheelchair, and not a writer."

Case smiled at him. "And do people stop trying to push you around once you get older?"

"There's a few who'll still try," Buddy said, "but mostly it's more that when you're older, you start seeing yourself through your own eyes, not someone else's. So what other people want you to be doesn't hurt as much."

"I hope so," Case said. "It's tough for now, though. Like I hate how I have to sit back and watch my dad yell at my mom when we visit. He better not do it again, that's all—or scare Lily."

"Sounds like he's trying to mess with everyone."

"And that's a laugh," Case said, bitter. "He's in jail! They even tell him when to get up in the morning. But he still thinks he's the boss of everybody. The weird thing is, he's worse than when we

were all living together in Cherry Hill." His dad was hardly ever home then, he thought. But it was pretty neat sometimes when he was. Case remembered conversations, jokes—he and his dad had even built that skateboard ramp together.

"I guess he hopes he's the boss of you guys still, at least."

"Well, he's not. And he better not try anything this visit. I'm ready for him."

"You know what *my* mom used to say?" Buddy asked. *"Never trouble trouble, until trouble troubles you."*

"What's that supposed to mean?" Case asked.

"It means maybe the visit will go okay. Don't go there expecting the worst."

"But if the worst happens, I'm ready for it," Case said grimly.

"Not a bad attitude, pal. Hey, are you going to see Ned again anytime soon?"

"Next week, probably. Why? Did he leave something here?"

"No. I just thought he might like a game of chess. I'm pretty good, you know."

"You are? Could you teach me to play better?" Case asked, suddenly shy.

"I didn't know you were interested, Case. Sure

I could teach you. I'd love having another chess player nearby."

"If I can even learn. Then I'll be able to add it to my list of killer accomplishments," Case joked. "Antiques, drawing, and chess."

"Don't knock it," Buddy said. "Judging from your most recent performance, I'd say you have the makings of a master plotter. You're a natural, Case."

"I guess," Case said, thinking of playing chess with Ned—and Ellie. "Yeah, I can kind of see it!"

As he climbed the stairs to his apartment, Case found himself remembering the family's first visit to Southwark Penitentiary, last summer. Parts of it had been awful—waiting, signing in, being searched by the man with the metal detector, even having the picnic basket searched—but there had been some good things, too.

Such as the sight of his dad's familiar face as he walked toward them...

And Lily's gap-toothed smile when she saw her father again...

And even his dad's own words: "The thing I resent most," he'd whispered privately to Case, "is being taken away from you and Lily. Especially

you, Case. A boy needs a father. You need *me*. I—
I'm sorry, kid."

Case hadn't been able to say a word in reply.

Then his dad said, "Thanks for bringing them,"
to Case's mom. "Hey," he added, turning to his
children, "I love you guys."

"I love you too, Daddy," Lily said, and she
started to cry.

"Me too," Case had said. "I love you too."

Maybe today wouldn't be as bad as the
Christmas visit was, Case thought as he slowly
turned the doorknob. Well, how could it be?
Maybe Buddy was right—he shouldn't go there
expecting the worst. He would give it a chance.

Case opened the door and saw Lily, surrounded
by feathery drifts of torn paper. He saw his mother,
talking on the phone to one of her friends. She
looked up and smiled at him.

*I'll be ready this time*, he thought. *For whatever
happens.*

## EPILOGUE

"It's me. I know you guys aren't home yet—hey, you only left a few minutes ago! I miss you already, though, so here's a special hug for my Lily-baby. I guess I just wanted to tell you, thanks for coming—I know this place stinks. But everything went okay, didn't it? Considering?"